NOTHING *happens* BY CHANCE

Armour

JUDY ROGERS

Nothing Happens by Chance

© Judy Rogers 2025

Published by Armour Books
P. O. Box 492, Corinda QLD 4075 Australia

Cover images: StudioDec12 | Etsy; Mick Haupt | Unsplash

Interior art: askib, Marinka, Morphart, alina.ill.mail.ru | DepositPhotos; microvectorone | Creative Fabrica

Interior design and typeset by Beckon Creative

ISBN: 978-1-925380-88-0

 A catalogue record for this book is available from the National Library of Australia

Endorsement

JUDY HAS A FANTASTIC imagination and reads between the lines of Scripture with great insight and creativity. Her stories enhance and bring the Bible narrative to life with a fresh perspective. To have a lifetime of experience, imagination and literature contained in one place is a real gift to all who will read this book.

— John Milburn

Lead Pastor — Brisbane West
iSee Church

NOTHING
happens
BY CHANCE

JUDY ROGERS

Contents

Foreword

SOME CHARACTERS HAVE A STORY to tell and don't stop nagging until it is told. Barabbas was one such character. Years ago, he started telling me his story. I wrote a bit then put him aside, and bought a new computer. But he kept nagging me so much, I fired up the old memory stick and let him talk. I guess he wanted more than anything to share the redemption of the cross, the power of repentance and the freedom of forgiveness.

'The Pharisee' talked to me for pages and pages until he revealed his name and identity. Now it's your turn to discover him.

Salome's intense loathing of her lot in life surprised me. My heart bleeds at her gilded-caged life, her desire for bare-footed friends and the horror of her mother's manipulation.

Some of you met Simon and Martha in *Palette of Grace*, but you haven't met Hadassa or Rhoda or Eliakim or Zed or Obadiah… and I bet you think you know everything about Bartimaeus. Think again. Let him tell you what happened after he was healed.

It never ceases to amaze me the way God gives us ideas and stories, stores them for years and then reveals them again at just the right time. He has crocheted lyrics from a music CD I recorded over 20 years ago into this book — the same words now portraying far more powerful meanings.

This book is filled with stories of biblical characters who may or may not have met Jesus. Some may not have even lived. Who knows? John says Jesus did so many things that there wouldn't be enough books in the world to record them. (John 21:25)

I may portray some characters in a very different light from what you have heard or learnt or studied. I'm sure you'll have the grace to open your imaginations and forgive me.

I pray you do. I pray you take Jesus out of the box you have put Him in.

I pray you see Him as the man He became — a strong influential leader, a storyteller, a fun-loving man, a family man caring enough for you to let

Himself be tortured and killed... powerful enough to rise from death.

I pray you'll find Him as your Lord and King, incomprehensible beyond measure, creator of all, forgiving, loving, the Lord of all creation — through Him all things were made and without Him nothing was made that was made.

I pray you'll join in the prayer of the disciples declaring your need for Him, your trust in Him, and declaring your faith in Him.

Our future can't be built
    without a past to build upon.

Our future can't be built
    without mentors true and strong.

Our future can't be built
    without decisions wise and true.

Lord, our future can't be built
    without You.

— Judy Rogers

The Plan

Our God works in mysterious ways.
I'll never forget that.
And neither should you.
His plans were set in motion
Before time began.
I can't express how humble I feel
to be part of the most amazing plan
ever planned.

The Plan

CLOPAS' LITTLE HANDS TREMBLED under mine... so tiny, so small, so frail, fluttering like the wings of a butterfly. Was I ever that small? Even my fourteen-year-old-hands — childish compared to our abba's, engulfed his. Abba's big weathered hands can envelop us all like over-sized mittens... like the hands of a giant... like his father's hands. I miss Grandfather.

I often hear adults say, 'Where has time gone?' I'm beginning to think the same. Maybe I'm growing up.

'Joseph, I'm ready.' A head of dark curls squirmed in front of me, entangling the scrawny stubble on my chin. I refocussed.

'Well done, Clopas,' I murmured over the top of his head. 'Now angle the plane down just so.'

He held his breath and let me guide his hands.

'I did it! Abba, come and see what we made,' he exclaimed in awe, watching his wood shaving spiral in a perfect coil and bounce to the floor. He bent down and scooped it up in both hands, then looked up at me with eyes full of wonder.

My heart smiled. I remember my first wood spiral when Abba held my hands just so.

Abba glanced from the wheel he was turning. 'Well done, Son. Well done!' He strode over to inspect the masterpiece, crushing hundreds of his own discarded shavings with his big feet on the way. 'My goodness, it won't be long before you're taking over the family business.'

'You're so funny.' Clopas' laugh was contagious. I loved the way my little brother's nose crinkled when he laughed. 'Joseph will be taking over the business.' He grinned at me.

'I'll need some good carpenters to help, though,' I smiled back. 'You don't think I'll be able to do it one my own, do you?'

Wonder swirled through his eyes. 'You mean you'll want me to help you?'

'This is a family business, Clopas. One day, it will be the biggest and best carpentry shop in all of Galilee. One day, everyone will know about it. One day, one of our sons will be the most famous carpenter in the world.'

I ruffled Clopas' hair and caught a look of pride on Abba's face.

'Oh, maybe,' Clopas added. His dancing eyes usually meant an idea was forming in his head. 'Maybe your son could be king.'

'What?'

'Well, we're from the line of King David, right?'

Abba and I stared at each other, wondering where this conversation was heading. Once Clopas started, he just kept going.

'So,' he added, without missing a beat. 'You're the oldest, Joseph. Your son could be king and my children and I will bow before him and call him "Lord". Everyone would call him "Lord".' Clopas spread his arms wide. 'He could save Israel ... maybe the world.'

'Clopas. Stop,' I chuckled. 'Let's not worry about our children. We're not even old enough to get married. Besides,' I added, ruffling his hair again, 'you don't even like girls. Remember?'

Abba cleared his throat. 'Come along, boys, I'm sure it is time for supper.'

Clopas caressed the spiral in his hand, world-salvation forgotten. 'Just one more, Abba, please? I need to practice so I can help Joseph.'

Abba's hearty laugh brought our minds back to the workshop. 'Just one more.'

I handed Clopas the plane and chuckled as he nearly dropped the heavy tool. 'Remember now,' I whispered. 'Watch the grain of the wood. Angle the plane — that's the way — brace your legs — now push.'

A small perfect shaving spiralled down to the floor. 'I did it all by myself!'

Abba nodded. 'Saba Eleazar would be most proud too. He taught me how to work wood when I was a boy like you. Most of these tools were his.'

I felt my throat constrict. 'I miss Saba Eleazar.'

'So do I, Son. So do I.' Abba cleared his throat. 'Help me put the tools away and we'll show Amma how clever Clopas has become.'

I steered my little brother into the main room of our modest dwelling. Both his hands were cupped, holding his precious spirals, like baby birds.

Amma looked up from the dough she was kneading and inspected the little coils of wood. She smiled a wondrous smile. 'These are amazing! You should be most proud.'

She was once a beautiful woman, but an attack by a Roman soldier had left her with a scar on her forehead. She limped when she was tired and needed to rest often. She snuggled under Abba's outstretched arm. 'It won't be long before you're as clever and strong as your abba. Now go and wash — all of you! Supper is ready. Then we're going to visit Anne and Joachim. They have a new baby girl.'

Clopas pulled a face. 'A baby girl!'

'Yes,' Amma laughed. Her brown eyes danced. 'A girl. They've called her Mary. You never know, you might grow up to be friends one day.'

Clopas rolled his eyes at me and we both snorted in fits of giggles.

The water in the well was cold, even though it was mid-summer. 'I like Anne and Joachim,' I said, scrubbing my arms.

Joachim was taller than Abba and wore the same long beard. He was just as much fun to be around, although somewhat older. Like our parents, Anne and Joachim worshipped and loved the one true God. Our families went to the temple together, built our sukkot shelters together and shared a Passover lamb.

'I do too,' Clopas answered, testing the cold water. 'I like the way Anne's eyes sparkle when she talks. She's always happy.'

I was looking forward to venturing out at night. Somehow a night-time visit seems a bit more exciting... even dangerous … almost like an adventure.

'Do you think Abba will let me carry the lantern, now that I'm going to be a carpenter?' Clopas asked.

'Maybe,' I chuckled.

Clopas stopped scrubbing his hands and looked up at me. 'How could this happen?'

I stared back, confused.

He rolled his eyes and shook his head in dismay. 'A girl! Why couldn't they have had a boy?

I grinned at his melodramatics. 'I don't think they had any say in it really, Clopas. And it's not as if you have to marry her or anything... You have to admit, though, Mary isn't a bad name.'

'Yeah, for a girl!'

Was My Father Right?

God's plans never fail.
He promised a Messiah.
Centuries pass.
Those of the faith search and pray in hope and faith.
And die.
More faithful are born,
More search and pray in hope.

God's plans never fail.
He promised a Messiah.
He came.
Some recognise Him,
And are blessed with a life of freedom,
And praise to God for His promise kept.
A life of joy and redemption.
Yes, some recognise Him,

How sad for those who don't.

Was My Father Right?

EVERY MORNING, AND EVERY EVENING, for as long as I can remember, my father retreated to the rooftop to pray.

When he became too old to negotiate the stairs, he found a comfortable place under an acacia tree in the courtyard. Most mornings, before I set out for the synagogue, I prayed with him. Every time it was the same. He beseeched God to let him see the Messiah before he died. Every morning he woke, so I guessed the Messiah hadn't come in the night.

I've read the scriptures.

I've studied the scriptures.

I believe the scriptures.

I know God's word is true.

I know our Messiah will come.

Ever since I was a boy, Father taught me and encouraged me to find answers for myself. To search the texts, to cross-reference, to explore options. I've taught my students to do the same.

Most evenings, before bed, my little son sat on Father's lap, listening to the wonders of the Sacred Words — the words Father taught me, when I was young. Father's eyes were now too dim to read, but he recited the prophets and Psalms with passion. I listened too, never tiring of hearing God's promises about the coming Messiah. I named my elder son Simeon after my father. He is only two, so too young to really understand. I pray he'll find the truth.

'Keep your eyes open, lad,' Father said over and over to my boy. 'He'll be about your age.' One night Father gripped my hand. 'Open your eyes, too, Gamaliel. It won't be long. Look for Him. He'll show the real way to life.'

For a few months, Father wore a secret smile and my spirit roiled with unexplainable anticipation. Something was in the air.

'Gamaliel,' Father called one morning. 'I'd like to go to the Temple with you today.'

It wasn't an unusual request but, for some reason, this morning, my spirit leapt. Why, I didn't know. There was nothing remarkable about the morning sun or the breakfast we had shared. The only extraordinary thing was the fact that father had risen to his feet unassisted, combed his hair and was waiting for me at the gate. His cloak flowed behind him, stirring the dust. A sudden sadness passed over me. Father no longer stood strong and tall. 'Come along, Gamaliel,' he called.

When we arrived at the Temple, the prophetess, Anna greeted us with open arms. She was eighty-four, a widow and a true worshipper, who spent her time here in the Court of the Women serving God. I detected an unspoken excitement in her spirit too.

Determined to stay close, I watched. I watched my father. I watched Anna. I watched the crowd. People milled around. People approached with offerings. People headed in to pray — nothing out of the ordinary was happening.

A young couple arrived, baby in arms. I smiled. Father and Anna swivelled towards each other. A strange look passed between them. Their faded eyes sparkled with a sudden unspoken secret. Then, old age forgotten, as if performing an unrehearsed dance, they moved as one towards the young couple.

Father reached for the baby.

The parents looked confused.

My father's words shocked me, encouraged me, brought me to tears.

'Lord, now You are letting Your servant
depart in peace:
according to Your word.
for my eyes have seen Your salvation
which You have prepared before
the face of all peoples.
A light to bring revelation to the Gentiles
and the Glory of Your people Israel.'

The baby didn't take his eyes from my father's.

Father looked to heaven and blessed the parents too. He held the baby close and spoke to the mother. *'Behold, this child is destined for the fall and rising of many in Israel, and for the sign which will be spoken against you — yes, a sword will pierce your soul also — that the thoughts of many hearts may be revealed.'*

Still the baby watched my father's face — His gaze almost saying He understood every word.

Anna caressed the baby's cheek. He smiled and grasped her wrinkled finger. She stroked his brow and gave thanks to the Lord, telling those gathered around to look to the baby for redemption in Jerusalem.

The couple stared at Anna and Father in wonder — almost as if they knew something no one else did.

Less than a week later, Anna's old heart stopped. Her mission on earth complete, her eternity just begun.

For the next two months, Father's smile didn't waver. He urged little Simeon to search for the truth and implored me to keep an eye out for the young couple.

We said goodbye to Father one cold morning. His old body was buried; his spirit set free.

Through discreet inquiries, I discovered the family was from Galilee and had travelled to Bethlehem for the census, where the baby was born. A baby of the lineage of David born in Bethlehem!

> *'But you, Bethlehem, in the land of Judah, are not the least among the rulers of Judah. For out of you shall come a Ruler who will shepherd My people, Israel.'*

I remember sitting, staring at that Scripture until my eyes watered.

His birth caught the attention of other seekers as well. Magi from the east came to Jerusalem to pay homage to a king whose star they had seen in the sky.

It seems I was not the only one on the trail. They, however, were looking for a king. I was looking for the Messiah. Herod of course was jealous, but no one could have ever guessed the depths of depravity his rage would take him. Bethlehem's innocent baby boys lost their lives because of his greed, his envy, his insecurity.

My heart grieved… grieved for the babies, for their parents, for their grandparents, for their siblings, for destinies unfulfilled. I grieved for our land. I grieved we were ruled by hatred. I grieved we were ruled by idol worshippers. Their idols were power and riches.

I had to remind myself over and over, if the baby my father and Anna prophesied over was the Messiah, God would protect Him and He was not drowned in the river with all the other little ones.

I prayed for the child every day.

It was thirteen years before I saw Him again. I recognised His parents, though the strapping young dark-haired lad, of course, looked nothing like the baby my father had held. Every time I close my eyes, I see Him snuggled in my father's arms, dark hair poking under the edge of His homespun woollen blanket, little pink lips pursed. It's an image I often savour. I know the words my father said by heart.

I watched the boy and repeated my father's words under my breath.

Nothing seemed out of the ordinary. Jesus ran about with the other boys, eating as much as He could, teasing His brothers, reciting Scripture with ease.

After the feasting, the travellers left for their long walk home. I went back to the Temple to give thanks. There, to my surprise, the lad, Jesus, sat with the elders. His answers amazed me. I stood back to listen. More than His answers, His questions! Some stumped even the most learned. Some stumped me.

I watched and listened, overawed and every time I tried to reason it out, I came to the same conclusion… No little boy could have such knowledge, such concentration, such wisdom, such intimate understanding of the ways of God… unless…

… my father was right.

Based on Luke 2:25–47

Trust Me

Never have I had to
Delve into my being so deep.
Never have I had to trust,
To believe,
To have such faith in anyone before.
My life depended on obedience.

Exactly what He did,
Or rather, how He did it defies reason.
Yet, this strange man,
This man I watched grow up,
Defies reason.
Defies disobedience.

Trust Me

A WEDDING IS A WONDERFUL THING. A busy time though, especially for servants.

This wedding was inevitable. These families have eaten together, played together, built sukkot together, laughed together and cried together. Now it's time for Martha to leave our nest and join with Nathan. I feel honoured to be helping Nathan's servants with the planning and preparation. I guess they know me well enough to know I'd help anyway.

Jude was adamant his youngest sister's wedding house would be perfect. He and Nathan spent days poring over plans and months building. Being a carpenter's family has certainly helped in that regard. It's been finished for two weeks. Nothing left to the last minute. Jude is like that. His attention to detail is particular — annoying sometimes.

The family carpentry shop has no rivals here in Nazareth. It's been an established icon for nearly thirty years. Dependable, honest and affordable. Furniture, farm tools, carts, wagons, crucifixion beams roll out the door in high demand. It's usually Jude who completes the final details. He even sands the crucifixion beams, says stopping the splinters is the least he can do for the poor wretches.

Martha is the youngest of the girls and the first to be married since their father, Joseph, died. This is going to be hard on Mary. I keep an eye on her but, as usual, she holds her head high and smiles, her inner strength reflecting her faith.

I have been with this family for twenty-five years. I've watched the children grow. Watched James, Joses and Jude marry and bounce children on their knees, watched Salome through her pregnancies. Watched her bury her first-born. Watched her juggle her twins.

Watched Jesus.

Ever since He was a boy, there's been something extraordinary about Him — His walk, His eyes. It's almost as if He could see right into your soul. Now He's a man—a strange man in many ways, gentle but firm, wise but vulnerable. I believe He's been chosen by God to do something amazing. I don't know what — but something.

Martha is as beautiful as we expected. We all spent hours together stitching her gown and wedding veil with beads and embroidery.

The celebration is perfect — although I may be a little biased.

The food is perfect — I may be a little biased there too.

Then comes the whisper no one wants to hear — the whisper everyone dreads. Mary clasps Jesus' arm. Her eyes hold the agony of the truth. 'They've run out of wine.'

He shakes His head. 'Woman, what has it to do with Me? My time has not yet come.'

A strange answer from a strange man.

Only Mary can hold his gaze. She squeezes His arm and turns to me. 'Whatever He says to you, do it.'

A twitch of a smile plays on Jesus' lips. He looks back at His mother, takes a deep breath and gives her a slight nod. Turning to me, He orders the six stone water jars to be filled.

They don't want water. They want wine.

I dare not protest aloud, but my insides are screaming. Even though I have patched His scraped knees and rubbed His bruises for twenty-five years, I must obey. Then, I see the look in His eyes — a mysterious look — a look I've never seen before. For a moment our eyes lock and He gestures towards the jars.

Mystified, I set the younger servants to the task and step back. Pail by pail, fresh cold water is tipped into the jars until they overflow. The servants look to me. I nod and they scurry away.

Jesus looks to the roof, closes His eyes and puts His hands right into one of the pots. He smiles, looks to the roof again and beckons me. 'Draw some out and take it to the master of ceremonies.'

Are you kidding me? Take a pot of water to the master of ceremonies? My face must have betrayed me.

'Trust Me,' Jesus whispers.

Based on John chapter 2

Why did I Do It?

Why is guilt so painful?
How can something in your mind
cause physical pain?
But it does.
Shame,
Guilt.
Fear.
But I learnt how to evict them.
I met the man Jesus.
I let Him fight my battle.
And He won.

Why did I Do It?

I HAVE NEVER DESPISED ANYONE as much as I despise myself.

I didn't mean to kill the man — just rough him up. I thought it was just a travel bundle the woman with him was holding. What if I'd succeeded in ripping it from her arms? What if I'd thrown it on the ground as I intended?

It was a baby!

A baby!

I grip my hair and curl into a ball at the memory.

No wonder the man tried to protect his wife. No wonder he tried to protect the bundle — it was a baby!

And I killed him for it.

An innocent man lost his life.

A young woman lost her husband, her protector, her provider.

And a baby will never know its father.

All because I was an arrogant fool, trying to prove my worth as a legionnaire. The others laughed, congratulated me. 'Just one less Jew,' they mocked.

I don't know where my mind went. Into attack mode, I guess. I completely lost control. The taunts from the men... the initiation ritual... 'Rough someone up and steal their belongings.'

I never wanted to be a soldier. I wanted to paint. I wanted to sculpt, to create a mosaic. I still have a beautiful pattern running around my head. It would have been a masterpiece.

My servant, Barak, is the only one who understands and the only one I've shared with. We've spent hours traipsing around Jerusalem discovering architecture and works of art. That was before I turned sixteen.

I had two choices then — well, I really didn't have any choice. My father made the decision for me. Either I was conscripted or I followed him into the military. No choice really. Either way, I lost my dream. Instead, I'll spend the next sixteen years fighting against becoming my father.

I grew up in a household with a father who brought his military discipline home. My mother spends her days running the household with order and precision. She has slaves to command, ensuring her parties are no less well-organised than my father's parades. I have three spoilt younger sisters. At least none of them will have to face life as a soldier. I hope they'll never have to spend their lives married to one.

Agony

I find a little one-man-sized niche in the outer stone wall of the barracks. It's my solitude spot. My safe haven. Although nowhere is safe from the memories that plague me, stalk me, trying to grip my sanity. The woman's shriek of anguish echoes through my head, day and night, haunting me, taunting me. The man's blood covers her hands. The baby's cry joins her screams. I remember staggering away. I remember the other recruits laughing.

I grip my stomach, trying to hold my emotions to no avail. My gut explodes into a roar of torture, leaving me panting in a foetal ball.

I had watched the man's funeral procession from a distance. The poor young woman needed to be held up — carried almost.

How would she live now? How would she provide for her child? It's my fault.

I lean back against the outside wall of the barracks. A plan etches its way around my brain. I count up my coins and make my way into the marketplace.

Half an hour later, with a basket full of fruit and bread and a few coins at the bottom, I make my way to the address I have been given. I realise what a dumb idea it is. A Roman soldier in the Jewish quarters carrying a basket of food. Too late now. Hoping I have the right house, I leave the basket on the doorstep and hightail it away.

I'll have to find an accomplice for my next delivery and I think I know just the one. Barak, my servant, holds so many of my secrets, one more won't make any difference. I plan my next secret delivery.

Sweaty nightmares wake me every night. My screams wake the others in the barracks. Dark shadows circle my eyes. Hollow cheeks haunt my face.

I'm ordered to see the commanding officer — my father.

I wait a full minute outside his door, summoning up the courage to announce my presence. He sits behind his desk. I look up from the floor. Something is different. Something is almost... gentle in his eyes. It's not my father's usual power-hungry eyes that meet mine. Does he know what I did? Of course he does — he knows everything. It's his job.

More worrying... does he know how it has affected me? Of course he does — he knows everything. It's his job.

More worrying still... does he know about the basket of food I gave the widow I created? I hope not.

'Have a seat, Son,' Father says.

Son? He hasn't called me 'son' for years. I sit and wait with pounding heart.

'There is a centurion in Capernaum who is looking for another soldier.' He pauses. 'I'm sending you.'

I gulp. *Capernaum?*

Father continues with a voice I've only heard him use with Mother. Almost gentle. 'I believe things have been difficult for you here. Forcing someone into initiation challenges is an act of stupidity. The culprits have been dealt with.'

My ears burn. *He knows.* I stare at my hands.

'Aelius, sometimes a change of scenery helps.'

I dare look up, but wish I hadn't. I've never seen his eyes full of compassion — ever. Mine fill.

'You're to report to Capernaum in three days.' Father stamps a letter and hands it to me. Back to business, as usual.

I stand and salute. 'Yes, Sir.'

'Go home for a couple of days, Aelius. You need some rest and some decent food.'

I frown. I can't help it. 'Yes, sir.' I mumble and leave with a thousand more emotions swirling than I had before. But home sounds like a wonderful idea. Besides, it'll give me a chance to catch up with Barak and explain my plans. I'm pretty sure he'll revel in the conspiracy.

Capernaum, By the Sea.

The barracks here seem fresher than those in Jerusalem. Maybe it's the sea air. Something else feels fresher but I can't put my finger on it. I'm met with a smiling soldier who shows me to my bunk. He seems a decent sort of fellow but I don't let my guard down. I've made that mistake before.

'My name's Camillius. You're on third watch with me,' he grins. 'I'll take you to Centurion Gaius and wait for you. Watch starts in about an hour. We'll have time to grab a bite first.'

Is he really this friendly… or buttering me up for failure?

The Centurion's office surprises me. The window is wide open, filling the room with fresh sea air. The view of the water is stunning.

He stands and returns my salute. 'Welcome, soldier. We've teamed you with the third watch. You'll start in an hour. Your watch leader will inform you of our rules. Keep them — there are consequences.' He's a giant of a man with a voice like one of the sea monsters I've read about. His salute as crisp as a dried leaf. I doubt I'll want to find out what the consequences are.

A beaming Camillius meets me. Is his grin painted on?

I stare at our breakfast. Fish? Fresh fish and greens? Surely the soldiers here don't eat this well every day! We devour our food, straighten our uniforms and leave.

I follow Camillius up the road.

'We need to hurry,' he puffs. 'Don't want to miss the meeting.'

'Meeting? I thought we were reporting for third watch,' I puff back.

Camillius stops and turns. 'I guess nobody told you.'

My gut drops. 'Told me what?'

'We have the job of protecting a house.'

'A house,' I repeat. 'We're protecting a house?'

'Commander Gaius built it for a friend. A tax collector, named Matthew. The Commander was in charge of overseeing his work. One day Matthew up and left his job to follow a new teaching.'

'And he was so happy he built the man a house?'

Camillius chuckled. 'Gaius was impressed with the teaching — not Matthew. Apparently, he has great respect for their leader. He works miracles. Heals the sick and such.'

Things were getting weirder every minute. I've heard of this sect, led by a rebellious man ... stirring up the Pharisees, teaching — well, I don't actually know what he's teaching, but apparently, it's violating their law. Seems the only thing they can agree on is that everything is controlled by one God. One God? Everyone knows there is more than one God. Ceres is the goddess of agriculture and Minerva gives us wisdom.

I frown. 'We're going to their meeting? And they're going to let us in?'

'We don't actually attend the meeting. We stand behind a curtain and listen.'

'Intriguing,' I mutter. 'It sounds like a pretty simple watch.'

Camillius nods. 'Probably will be today, but rumour has it, their leader will be in town next week. That'll bring out the crowds and, no doubt, riots.'

My first sight of the house floors me. It's more like a mansion compared with the other houses in this small fishing village. We arrive after a fifteen-minute jog. Our uniforms are heavy with sweat. The house is two-storied with a barred entrance gate where a Roman soldier stands guard. He nods us through.

I can't help but stare around. A covered central courtyard is surrounded by wooden archways. Sheer curtains float between them in the breeze. About two dozen people, dressed in common attire, sit on benches in front of a grey-bearded man reading from a scroll. He looks up and raises his hand. Camillius acknowledges his greeting and pushes me behind the curtain. We're the only two soldiers on this side but I imagine there are two on each of the other three sides of the courtyard. Doors leading to who knows where are closed behind us.

I turn my attention to a new speaker although I know I'm not going to be the least bit interested. The only thing well-kept about him seems to be his beard.

'I tell you,' he says, 'I was paralysed.' His voice catches.

I peer through the curtain.

Paralysed? He's not paralysed.

'My friends here...' He gestures to some scruffy men in the front row. '... had the faith I didn't have. They carried me to the top of the house and tore a hole in the roof.'

Gasps fill the air. Mine maybe included.

'Then,' continues the man, 'they lowered me down on my mat right a Jesus' feet. I tell you...' He smiles, eyeing his friends. '... to be so vulnerable... to have your life in the hands of others is a very humbling thing.'

'What happened?' one man verbalises my mental question.

The speaker takes a deep breath. 'Jesus said, "Your sins are forgiven you."' He closes his eyes then stares at his feet. 'You people only know half of what I've done.' His voice peters out. He takes another steady breath. 'Jesus knew it all. How… I don't know. In that instant, power surged through my legs.'

'And the Pharisees didn't object?' someone calls.

'Of course the Pharisees objected,' the man chuckles. 'But just to prove Jesus has the power to forgive sins, He said to me, "Get up. Pick up your mat and go home."'

Everyone claps and the scruffy friends surge forward to slap the man on the back. I don't know how their kippahs stay on their unkempt hair.

My day is getting weirder.

Singing erupts. I'm guessing it's some sort of hymn. I glance at Camillius. He's grinning, which is nothing new, but he's also swaying to the music. The song ends and refreshments are served. I'm guessing it's time to leave but then a servant appears and gives me a plate of dates. I thank him and watch Camillius say something to the servant. They both laugh. The rest of the morning follows a similar format. Someone speaks. Someone prays. They all sing. They eat. We eat. I'm surprised when Camillius touches my arm and indicates the door.

'That's the weirdest watch I've ever had,' I confess on our way back to the barracks.

'Pretty awesome, hey!'

'And you believe it all?'

Camillius stops and looks me in the eye. 'Yes. Yes, I do.' He turns and leaves me standing flabbergasted, in the middle of the road.

A note awaits me when I arrive at the barracks.

Hadassa and baby Rhoda are well.

Instructions going according to plan.

Rhoda — so the baby is a girl. Another punch of guilt pounds my gut. 'Hadassa, I'm so sorry,' I whisper.

And so begins my life in Capernaum. Watches at the big white house continue. Nights are tormented by Hadassa's screams. Now I know her name, it makes it harder to bear. I wish I could have the peace the people in the big white house seem to have. I can honestly say I'm impressed by their genuineness. Sometimes they share stories. Always they pray. Always they sing. I actually found myself humming along yesterday.

Today, though, there's excitement in the air. I feel it the moment I wake. Something is different. Something is about to happen. Camillius' smile is even wider than before — if that's at all possible.

Gaius strides around the parade ground like a lion — intent, powerful, expectant. 'Double up on watches today,' he orders. 'No heroics.'

My heart jumps. *Is he talking to me?*

'Don't step in unless you're needed,' Gaius' voice booms away. 'Just our presence should be enough. Double at the house. You know what to do.'

I don't have a clue. I am counting on Camillius to fill me in.

Our watch is stationed at the city gates. We hear the crowd before it surges onto the streets. I tense. Camillius holds my arm. 'Relax, Aelius.' His eyes are shining.

The mob arrives, but it's not a mob of violence. It's a mob of joy, of cheering, of laughter. No issues here. I relax until I see the look in the eyes of the priests. If anger could burn the air, we'd all be gasping for breath. I nudge Camillius and track my eyes towards them. He follows my gaze. 'They won't do anything yet,' he says. 'They're out to find fault.'

We follow the crowd towards the house where Jesus enters with forty or fifty people.

Then a strange thing happens. People flock to the gates carrying sick on stretchers. People leading the blind. People with bandages and slings. People holding children and assisting the elderly.

I frown.

'It's always like this,' Camillius raises his voice above the clamour. 'They want to be healed.'

'You mean we'll see Him do it?' I am incredulous.

Camillius chuckles. 'Just stick around, my friend, and watch the love of the God of the universe.'

I have no answer.

Our uniforms are beginning to cook us, so we find a patch of shade. My heart goes out to the poor wretches standing in the sun. *What if they don't get healed? What if it's all a hoax?*

A cheer erupts. Camillius drags me forward. 'Watch,' he whispers.

People reach towards Jesus. He stops and touches everyone. My eyes cannot comprehend what I see. Lame walk. Blind see. Children, mothers, fathers, grandparents. Nobody leaves. Laughter and singing explode. People dance in the street.

Jesus looks up and locks eyes with me. My heart explodes. He strides towards me. Does he know I killed Hadassa's husband? He puts His hands on my head. 'Peace, Son. Guilt, I command you to leave this man. Shame begone. You have no more right to be here.' I fall to the ground in a wave of wonder. He kneels beside me. 'There's nothing you can do to change things, Aelius, but My Father in Heaven sees how you are helping Hadassa. I'm proud of you.'

I stare at him. 'How…?'

'On your feet, soldier,' Jesus orders.

I try to rise but fall back again. Camillius hoists me up. 'Don't worry,' he says. 'I'm not going to ask any questions.'

We follow Jesus back down the street, the crowd swirling around us. My heart is soaring. My head is fuzzy. My chest is free. Camillius pulls me to a stop.

Gaius? Commander Gaius is kneeling in front of Jesus. 'Please,' he whispers. 'My servant is lying at home paralysed and dreadfully tormented.'

Jesus raises him to his feet. 'I will go and heal him.'

'Lord,' the Commander answers. 'I am not worthy that You should come to my house, but just speak the word and I know he will be healed. For I am also a man who has authority. I say to one soldier, "Go", and he goes. To another, "Come", and he comes. Just say the word.'

Jesus smiles and grips Gaius' arms. 'I tell you, I have never found such great faith anywhere. Go your way, Gaius, and let it be done just as you believe.'

Lord? Did Commander Gaius just call this man 'Lord'? Surely that's blasphemy! Caesar is our Lord! I glance around, expecting a sea of hostile faces but I just find a grinning Camillius. 'Watch the love of the God of the universe,' he whispers.

What sort of man is this Jesus, that even the most powerful man in the town kneels at His feet?

Based on Matthew 8:5-13

Mama Bear

There is nothing as fierce
As the love of a protective mother.
Nothing as ferocious
As a mother denied
The rights of her child.
Poor though we were,
Outcast though we were,
Shunned though we were,
My child would receive her blessing.

Mama Bear

WIDOWS ARE JUST ABOUT THE LOWEST in the pecking order. Widows with babies even lower. I can see everyone's looks… hear their thoughts. A single, young woman with a baby! Most don't look past that… don't see the distraught young widow… the desperate loneliness… the grief.

I gather up my resolve and what dignity I have left and hoist my little daughter onto my hip. Nobody's going to push this Mama Bear around. Not this time!

The man, Jesus, is in town. Stories always swirl around strangers, I know, but this man sounds different. The stories of Him make my heart race… and He's so near, I can see His face, His eyes, His smile. Clutching Rhoda closer, I sidle around the outskirts of the crowd. I just want a blessing for her. Malachi didn't get a chance to bless his own daughter. Not before that Roman …

A blessing from Jesus would be the closest thing to a blessing from a father.

'Move away!' One of His disciples tries to shoo us like flies.

'No, Philip!' Jesus replies. 'Let the little children come to Me.' His gentle command held the power of storm-lashed waves.

Influential women, their head scarves long and coloured, crush ahead. Pushing their children towards Him. I wonder if they really looked into His face? Did they see His smile? Did they feel their hearts draw near for their children... or for themselves? I shunt the ugly thoughts away.

Tears well. Tears of frustration and anger and grief and desperation. What's the use of trying to get closer? Clutching Rhoda to my chest, I wrap my thin mantle around us both and lean against a post. I let the tears fall.

What's the use?

A shudder of resolve wakens me. Rhoda has as much right to be here as any of them.

The crowd stops churning. I look up. His eyes meet mine. Unfathomable love calls me. For some unexplainable reason, the crowd parts … silent for a change.

He reaches towards me… His smile so… beautiful… genuine… personal. 'Come.'

I swivel around to see who He's talking to … no one is behind me.

'Come, Hadassa.'

How does He know my name? In a dream I walk towards Him. To this day I still can't remember how. Jesus takes Rhoda into His arms. His blessing as rich as any a father could give.

Then He draws me closer. 'And bless this powerful Mama Bear too.'

Based on Mark 10:13–16

Hands of a Child

When you hold the hand of a child of today
You hold a heart in your hand.
And when you hold the heart of a child of today,
You hold the world in your hands.

One little hand will be a farmer.
One little hand will feed the poor.
One little hand will be a doctor.
One little hand will live next door.

One little hand is tomorrow's technology.
One little hand will uphold the law.
One little hand will build our machinery.
Pray that machinery will not be for war.

Today's little hands hold the future
of the nations.
Today's little hands hold tomorrow's peace.
Plant in those hands, tolerance and patience.
Plant understanding and wars will cease.

When you hold the hand of a child of today
You hold a heart in your hand.
And when you hold the heart of a child of today,
You hold the world in your hands.

Teach those little hands to love.
Teach those little hands to love.

Teach those little hands to love and respect.

Listen with Your Heart

I *don't think you can actually see*
anything
until you are
blind.

Listen with Your Heart

ONE THING ABOUT BEING BLIND is that you hear a lot... an awful lot. There's always gossip — some can make your hair curl — plotting and planning and cussing and crafty conspiracies and... whispers of love... and of course, there's always news.

Nobody takes much notice of me — the blind beggar everyone thinks is not quite right in the head. I've been here as long as most people can remember — part of the landscape. I can pull my dusty beggar's shawl over my head and melt into a building, a tree, a wagon. Nobody sees me, but I listen... and I hear.

That's what happened the day my life changed.

I sat, as usual, on the road outside Jericho. An inexplicable excitement quickened my heart. An inexplicable feeling clung in the air. I strained to hear what people were saying, how they were walking. Nothing seemed different.

But something *was* different.

Something was about to happen.

The animals were unsettled. Horses tossed their heads. Even the old dog who sat with me day by day lifted her head and sniffed the wind.

Yes, something was about to happen... an earthquake? A raid? I clutched my shawl and crept closer to Jericho's stone wall.

The ground rumbled. Feet rushed past. People shouted. Stalls snapped shut. I leaned closer against the wall and I listened. I listened with my inner sense, and I knew... I knew *He* was here. I have no idea how I knew. I couldn't see, but I could feel... and I knew.

Jesus of Nazareth was here.

I'd heard stories while I crouched under my shawl, melded to the rocks. If the villagers knew I'd been listening, I'd have been beaten... again.

I heard how He healed Jairus' daughter and the woman who touched the hem of His prayer shawl... and the paralytic who was let down through the roof. I couldn't get enough of the stories. They filled me with hope and faith... and despair. I was a poor blind beggar. Blind as long as I can remember. I knew He could heal me... but would He? A ripple of hope simmered in my gut.

The shouts grew louder. People laughed and danced.

I staggered to my feet and cried out, 'Jesus, Son of David, have mercy on me.' I don't know what possessed me.

The crowd silenced with a collective gasp. I could feel their stares. I could sense their horror. I could hear their unsaid accusations.

Then the mob erupted.

'How dare you?'

'Who do you think you are?'

'Unclean! Unclean!'

'Get back in the gutter where you belong!'

I sensed the blow before it landed.

There was a time in my life when I would have crawled back under my shawl and waited for more blows, more jeering, more ridicule... but not today. Today, I stood tall and called again. 'Jesus, Son of David, have mercy on me.' My tears ran. My nose ran. My shoulders heaved. I raised my arms to where I thought He was. 'Please.'

Then everything went silent... the people, the animals, even the wind. I wondered if the world had been swallowed by a monster and left me behind to float alone, in my black pit of desolation, forever.

A sneer told me there had been no monster and I wasn't alone. 'He's not going to listen to you — you daft babbling beggar.'

'Bring him to Me.' A voice as powerful as thunder and as soft as a wildflower, filled the air, cutting the next snigger mid-sentence.

'Now you're in for it,' someone snorted.

Was I in trouble for being so brazen? Was I about to be beaten?

'Come.' The voice again.

In that instant, I knew. I knew He not only *could* heal me, but He *would* heal me. I threw off my beggar's shawl. I'd never need it again. I was going to see!

'Come, My friend.'

My limbs filled with strength from some inner source. My heart rumbled in fear. I stepped towards the beautiful voice.

He smelt like sunshine. 'What do you want Me to do for you?'

My throat closed over. My heart pounded. I could feel power radiating from the Presence in front of me. 'Rabbi,' I croaked and cleared my throat. My doubts dissolved. I stood tall. I knew my miracle was about to happen. I could feel it. 'Rabbi,' I repeated. 'That I may recover my sight.'

I felt Jesus' smile. I felt His pleasure. I felt His power envelop me in a wave of fragrant sweetness.

Colours swirled before my eyes. I dared not close them. I wanted to capture every second. I tipped my head to the sky. More colours and now shapes spun and danced. It was wondrous... glorious. I felt jubilant. Laughter I had not felt in years bubbled in my chest and overflowed.

Jesus laughed too. A rich beautiful contagious laugh. He held my arm, steadying me and still He laughed. 'Go your way. Your faith has made you well.'

His eyes, rich and dark and full of fire and life and joy, captivated me. I couldn't look away. He embraced me. I froze. Nobody had touched me for years. I was embarrassed. I smelt like the gutter and He smelt like a fresh country road, like the sun, like a stream, like... heaven. Jesus held me tight. 'Relax, Son. You're loved. You're precious.' He squeezed me in a father's embrace. 'Your faith has made you well,' He repeated. Holding me at arms' length, He winked, squeezed my shoulders and turned to join His followers.

No one had moved during the entire exchange. The crowd stood as one in shocked silence. Then eyes travelled to me, to Him, to me again and then to His retreating back.

How long I stood in the street, I don't know.

'Bartimaeus?' wheezed Caleb, the owner of the bakery, pushing through the crowd towards me. Caleb was one of the only people who looked out for me. 'Are you hurt?'

I turned.

He gaped and waved his hand in front of my face. I baulked.

'You can see!'

My stupid grin answered him. Together we held hands and danced, whooping and giggling like five-year-olds.

'Who is He?' Caleb panted.

'Jesus,' I whispered. His name felt like a breeze on my lips. 'Jesus of Nazareth.' I grinned. 'Caleb! I've met the Messiah!' I took a deep breath, glanced at my discarded beggar's shawl, and stared at the group of men in the distance.

'I don't know any more than that, but I'm going to find out.'

Based on Mark 10:46-52

The Pharisee

I'M A PHARISEE.

Son of a Pharisee.

Great-grandson of a Pharisee.

I've studied hard for years.

I'm proud of what I've achieved.

I love the Torah. I intend to keep it and ensure others
do as well.

My name is Simeon
named after my grandfather.

I watch in wonder.

A crippled man rises and walks.

And I know something as beautiful and as pure as
the healing of a crippled man has to be from God.

I listen to the teachers of the Torah argue it,
as they watch Him from afar.

There is no way I'm going to get involved in this.

I watch my father and realise with a start
he never takes part in such arguments either.

I catch his eye just as they call him,
'Gamaliel, what are your thoughts?'

I see his heavy sigh and sidle closer to hear his answer.

'A house divided against itself will fall,'
my father answers.

Rabbi Nicodemus nods and gives me a smile.
So, it's not just me.

I'm the youngest here, the junior if you like,
and I've been given a task.

I'm to keep an eye on this healer, listen to His
preaching, note His words, note His movements.

And report back.

However, the more I watch the man,
the more I listen, the more I hear,

the more I realise He's more than a prophet.

No prophet healed the sick as He does.

No prophet casts out demons as He does.

Some days, I want to cast off my black robes,
just like I saw the blind beggar in Jericho cast off
his beggar's shawl when he was healed.

Some days, I want to sit at His feet like His disciples.

Some days I want Him to bless me — to put His
hands on my head and bless me

like He blesses the children.

Some days I feel like a child listening to His wisdom.

'If someone asks you to carry his pack for a mile,

(I knew, we all knew, he was referring to the Romans),
carry it two,' Jesus said.

This makes me think. Sounds a bit subversive and weak.

Then I realise, by law, a Roman can only order you
to carry his pack for one mile.

After that, if you step further, the Roman can be charged.

He is very careful to run after you, red-faced, and
stop you if you go further.

Tables are turned.

Brilliant! Jesus is brilliant!

Jesus continues. 'If a man slaps you
with his right hand, turn the other cheek.'

This really stumps me. Why? Why ask for trouble?

I sit near the fire, watching the flames, pondering.

Then it hits me! To be slapped on the right cheek,
a man must be hit by the aggressor's left hand —
the unclean hand.

If you turn the other cheek — the left cheek —
the aggressor must use his right hand.

No Roman would do that to a Jew!
It would be admitting he was an equal.

I almost laugh aloud when I realised.

Jesus chuckles. 'I wondered how long
it would take you to figure that one out.'

By now, I have been accepted by some of the group,
around their fire at night.

They know I have been sent to watch — to spy.

We walk… Jesus preaches… Jesus heals.

We walk again.

In one town, we are invited to dine with
a Pharisee named Nathan.

Never have I felt so condemned.

Not that Jesus says anything to me personally,
but what He says is true, so true.

'Woe to you, Pharisees, for you love the best seats
in the synagogues and in the marketplaces.'

Images of Pharisees from Jerusalem in their long robes,
extra-long prayer shawls hanging to the ground,
heads lifted high, churn my gut.

Yes, He's right.

How could we be so arrogant?

My grandfather's teachings from the Torah
were of love, not selfishness or pride.

How did we Pharisees become so hypocritical?

There is a woman in one of the towns
who has been bent over for eighteen years.

Eighteen years!

I can't imagine the pain.

Jesus simply calls to her and says,
'Woman, you are loosed from your pain.'

How beautiful to see her stand.

How precious. The smiles. The praises to God!

Yet — the ruler of the synagogue condemns Him.
Condemns Him for setting a woman free from pain
on the Sabbath.

But He puts them to shame. 'Does not each one of
you take your donkey from the stall and lead it to
water on the Sabbath? So should this woman
who has been bound for eighteen years
be freed on the Sabbath.'

People flock to be healed and blessed.

More and more people join His group.

He teaches them how to pray.
That's a bit of an eye-opener. Our *Father?*

It takes me a few days, but I come to the realisation,
He is right. How could He not be?

God provides for us, watches us, heals us, leads us.
How could He not be a father?

I dread the next week when I am to return
to give my report.

This man is no threat — except to the arrogance
of those whose noses are so far up in the air,
they can't see — won't see — truth
when it walks into their world.

I have thought often, during the last few weeks,
about my grandfather, Simeon, my namesake —
of the times he took me on his knee and told me his
prayer to see the chosen one of God before he died.

Of the time he went to the temple and recognised Him
— knew Him.

'He is just about your age,' Grandfather said often,
smiling at me.

'Open your eyes. Look for Him. He'll show the way
to life.'

I stare across the fire and I know.

I know it's Him.

Maybe my father sent me on this mission for a
reason.

Maybe I will shed my robes of office.

What is an office of God,
if one does not do the will of God?

Maybe I'll stay.

A Lesson from the Woodcarver

I didn't realise that wanting
More of this
And more of that,
A bigger this and a better that,
Just proved to the world
I was just an ungrateful, greedy wretch —
Not satisfied with what I already had.
It was the woodcarver and his family
Who taught me the way to a true,
satisfied life.
It's not gold or trinkets or paintings —
they do nothing but collect dust.
It's not jewels or houses that will be sold
to the next greedy man after I die.
It's a life free from the burden of wanting
and desiring,
Of trying to prove my status to a world that
really doesn't care,
Trying to impress people who really
don't care.
A life free of locks and bolts and the fear
of being burgled.
Free from wanting and converting.
Free from greed.
Free.

A Lesson from the Woodcarver

The Woodcarver

SAWDUST GRITTED INTO my sleep-deprived eyes and burrowed into my beard, but I knew I had to keep sawing and sanding and chiselling and hammering. My time was running out. Reaching for another board, I checked the lantern... just enough time to start another.

Footsteps scuffed on the gravel outside. I clasped a hammer to my chest and slunk into the shadows.

Lantern light filled the doorway. 'Abe?'

My tension dissipated and I stepped out from behind the bench. 'Suzannah, why are you here?'

'I'm here,' Suzannah began. She cleared her throat. 'I'm here because you're here.' Tears spilled down her face. 'Abe, you haven't been in the house for days. The children are asking about you. You haven't touched me for weeks.' Her voice cracked. 'Is there someone you would rather be with?' She took a step forward.

I stepped back.

Suzannah turned to flee.

'Wait!' I called. 'Please... there's something I need to tell you.'

Suzannah stopped but didn't turn.

'Please.'

I could see her shoulders shaking. She turned, eyes streaming.

Without another word, I rolled up my sleeve.

'No!' she whispered, staring in horror at the bandage around my arm. 'No! You can't have leprosy. You can't!'

I closed my eyes, my breath shuddering as unsteadily as my heart. This was not the way I had intended to tell her. Actually, I had no idea how I was going to tell her. I waved my hand around my workroom. Five stools stood ready to sand. I moved to the back of the workshop and removed a sheet. Fifty finished stools, piles of axe handles and farm equipment took up most of the space.

Suzannah frowned. 'You made all these?'

'I'm not going to be able to hide this much longer,' I croaked, holding up my arm. 'The rosemary herbs seem to be keeping it at bay, but when summer comes... long sleeves will be out of the question. You're going to need an income when I go to the leper colony.'

'No!' Suzannah's cry rent my heart. She fell to the floor. 'No, Abe. I can't live without you!'

Her distraught face undid me. I wanted to hold her, but I couldn't. I wanted to tell her everything would be all right, but it wouldn't. I had to leave. I had to leave Suzannah and my children. I wouldn't see them grow up. Wouldn't see my daughter marry. Wouldn't hold my grandchildren. I looked at the things I had made. Who was I kidding? This wouldn't support my family for more than a few months. I buried my hands in my face and sank to the floor, craving to hold Suzannah, craving to be held.

I swiped my eyes. 'Suzannah, you've been recording the business numbers for years. The older boys are skilled carpenters. Eli is sixteen. He's just about old enough to take over the business. I've arranged for him to apprentice with Mordechai.'

'You told your brother?'

'No. He just thinks he's giving Eli some extra pointers and business skills. I know he'll apprentice Samuel when he finds out. And I can't keep Deborah out of the workshop even now. I know it's not a girl's place but she's got the patience and attention to detail neither of the boys have.' I looked deep into my wife's eyes. 'Suzannah, there's no one in the whole of Samaria I would rather be with than you. Remember that.'

She nodded and left the barn.

I sat hunched in a dismal blob.

Scratching on the door woke me. Suzannah, eyes red and puffy, arrived with blankets, bread and an earthenware bowl. Even before she lifted the lid, my mouth watered. 'I figure if you always use this bowl and I serve myself first and sit over here, we could at least eat together.'

My heart melted. How could I leave her?

Wintery mornings dissolved, giving way to spring. Bird calls and sunshine welcomed each morning, reminding me my time was up. As much as I loved the hotter weather, this year it heralded despair, desolation and ruin — for my family, for my home, for my life. Although the herbs eased the pain, my arm was now covered in bandages. I was careful to burn the old ones and use clean wraps every day. But there was no hiding the leprosy now. It was time to shed long sleeves. It was time for me to leave.

We decided not to make a big spectacle of my departure. I packed a bag, and headed out the door.

The children played their part and waved. Suzannah played her part and waved. I played my part and waved. As far as the village knew, I was going to visit my parents in north Samaria.

The Ruler

Sun streamed between the marble pillars in my courtyard. At this time of day, the sunbeams reflected in precise rhythm on my new water feature. Sprays of water danced on the lilies and played with the lotus flowers, creating rainbows in the mist.

I sat on my carved wooden seat marvelling at the newly crafted table I had just commissioned. It was perfect. A marble statue sat in the exact centre. I'd commissioned that too. My eye tracked up the breezeway. Under the marble archways, three more exquisite statues sat in the centre of three matching carved tables. The carpenter at the bottom of the hill was extraordinary. I know the tables were worth more than I'd paid, but I managed to talk him down. He's just a carpenter, after all. He said the pleasure of creating something so beautiful was extra payment enough. I guess that's why he's poor and I'm rich.

I stood and walked down the breezeway, stopping at the next statue. How long had it been since I bothered to look at these? I couldn't even remember what the third statue looked like or where I had bought it. But everyone with means owns statues.

'Why?' I asked the marble lion. 'Who even sees you?' I ran my hands through my hair. 'There has to be more.'

I called my servant, Uzziah, to bring my embroidered cloak. I needed to get out… to go for a walk… somewhere… away from the opulent surroundings I had created. Unseeing, I headed along the street. People scattered. Some bowed. Some backed into buildings. I hated that, but I didn't know how to stop it.

A cry arose from around the corner 'The Teacher is here!"

I'd heard about the Teacher. People said He had the answers to life itself. I patted my money belt. Maybe, I should ask for an appointment. A surge of people carried me around the corner. They weren't bowing to me now, weren't scurrying out of my way. Seems the excitement of the Teacher was far more important than me.

By the way the people had mobbed towards Him, I was expecting some pretentious well-dressed man.

Maybe I was looking at the wrong person. The man sitting on the rocks in the palm grove was dressed as a traveller. Although His tunic was well cut, there was nothing to distinguish Him from the everyday villagers. His words were comforting. 'Mercy' I could handle. 'Peace' — yes. I settled back. This was nothing new.

'Beware of covetedness.' My breath caught in my throat. My ears burned. 'For one's life does not consist of the abundance of things he possesses.' I tried to discreetly cover my burning face, imagining everyone's eyes on me.

Then He told a story about a certain rich man who had no more room to store all his possessions. I frowned. My mind wandered. Didn't I just buy a new table to hold my new marble statue?

I refocussed and caught the next part of His story. 'The rich man said, "I will build bigger barns."' My heart raced. Was He having a go at me? I missed the next bit, but apparently, God killed the rich man! My heart felt as if it had exploded and bounced over every rib.

'So is he who lays up treasure for himself and is not rich towards God.'

I breathed again. I know I'm rich towards God... aren't I? Doubts spiralled through my mind. I thought I'd automatically have eternal life. After all, I was rich — wealthy beyond any of these grubby merchants here. I attended the synagogue. I even had a new prayer shawl. But the way Jesus spoke, eternal life was something very different from that in my imagination.

I needed to know the truth, but there was no way I was going to show my ignorance in front of this crowd. I was a ruler. I was important. Every now and then, Jesus looked at me and caught my eye. I studied the trees, studied the ground, studied my nails. Someone brought Him a drink. He stood and turned to go, then spun and held my gaze.

Summoning courage and overriding embarrassment, I stepped forward. It was now or never. 'Teacher,' I implored. 'What must I do to inherit eternal life?'

It was almost as if He was expecting me to talk with Him. 'You know the commandments. Do not commit adultery. Do not steal. Honour your father and mother.'

I was a bit taken aback. 'Sir,' I answered. 'I have been doing all these things since my youth.'

Jesus nodded. 'You lack one thing.'

I frowned. 'What else is there besides the law?'

Jesus' eyes softened. 'Sell all you have and distribute the money to the poor and you will have treasure in heaven.' He smiled. 'Then come and follow Me.' He held my gaze until I had to look away. Then He squeezed my shoulder and left me standing dumbstruck in the middle of the road.

I don't know how long I stood there. People milled past. Chit-chat floated by. Laughter erupted. Were they laughing at me? I glanced up. No, some poor farmer was arguing with his stubborn donkey. It was as if I didn't exist.

Sell all you have? Are You serious?

I held my head high and walked home with as much dignity as I could muster. People bowed. An old woman tried to hobble out of the way. She looked up, terrified, tears filled her eyes. 'Sir,' she stammered.

I took a step towards her. She cringed. I dug into my money belt. 'Shalom, mother,' I whispered, placing some coins into her hands.

She stared at them as if they would bite. Shock contorted her face. Tears overflowed. She tried to bow but almost toppled. I closed her hands over the coins and smiled.

I felt jubilant.

I stumbled home and collapsed into my beautiful carved chair. Tears burned. My face burned. My marble statues blurred. My beautiful carved tables blurred. He was right. The Teacher was right. What was the use of all this? Who cared?

Determination surged through me. Before I could change my mind, I called my servant, Uzziah, and commanded him to wrap the statues and take them to the dealer. A strange look crossed his face. 'Then,' I said, 'sell the tables. Make sure you get a good price.' I knew my orders would be obeyed. Uzziah was the most trustworthy man I had ever met and I had a suspicion he followed the Teacher I had met today. Little things he said, little things he did — kindness, generosity — I'm not sure exactly. Uzziah was just different. I've known him all my life. He's more of a friend than a servant, if it's allowable to have a servant as a friend.

For the rest of the afternoon, I went from opulent room to opulent room, choosing opulent furniture and paintings, treasures and trinkets. Looking through fresh eyes, I realised their futility. I thought of the carpenter at the bottom of the hill. I thought of the meagre dinner he would have shared with his family because I had shortchanged him. What had he said? 'The pleasure of creating something beautiful is payment enough.' I tipped my head to the ceiling. What have I ever made for someone else? What beautiful things have I ever created?

By the time Uzziah returned with the money from the sales, I had accumulated a staggering number of beautiful, useless treasures. He stared in wonder. Joy sparkled in his eyes.

'Yes,' I whispered. 'I met your Teacher.'

Uzziah grinned. 'It is easier for a camel to go through the eye of the needle than for a rich man to inherit the Kingdom of Heaven,' he whispered.

'Where did you hear that?' My heart deflated. 'Then there's no hope for me.'

'It doesn't mean a rich man can't get there. He just needs to get on his knees and put God first.' He looked around at the treasures I had discarded. 'God has given you these riches to extend His kingdom. Am I correct in thinking you'd like me to sell them too?'

I nodded.

With the money from the sale of the tables in my purse, I swallowed my pride and headed down the hill. It was time to repay some debts.

Again, people bowed and moved out of my way. Stopping in the middle of the street, I called. 'Please do not bow to me. I am just a man. Bow only to God.' The shimmer of surprise tumbling along the street nearly knocked me over. People stared, watching me walk on. A murmur followed me down the hill.

When I arrived at the carpenter's shop, I was shocked. The once-well-cared for house looked dusty and sad. Frayed mats hung over the drying ropes. I knocked on the door, surprised at the shabbily dressed woman who answered. Her clothes hung loosely on her shoulders. Dark shadows framed her eyes. I wondered for a moment if I had the right house, but she recognised me. 'I'm afraid my husband cannot make any more tables.' She cleared her throat. Her eyes welled.

'I'm not here to ask for a table,' I answered. 'May I come in?'

The woman seemed to deflate.

'Amma?' called a young man. 'Who's there?' In an instant, a tall, dark-haired youth with the scratching of a beard stood behind the woman. 'Can I help you?'

'Please…' I glanced along the street at half a dozen busybodies. 'I have something to discuss in private.'

'Of course,' the young man answered with more honour than I know I deserved. I stepped over the threshold into a very different room from the one Uzziah and I had entered a year ago. A chipped bowl holding dried dates and half a loaf of bread sat on the hearth where a pot of lentils simmered. Another youth appeared, younger, with dancing eyes and a smile as broad as a chariot.

'I've come,' I stated, looking at those in the room, 'to ask your forgiveness and make restitution.'

Blank stares greeted me.

'Last year, I commissioned four carved tables. Most beautiful workmanship I have ever seen.'

The woman began to cry and I suspected her husband might have died. That would explain the deterioration of the once cared-for home.

'Abba is no longer able to work,' a young woman called from the back door. Sawdust clung to her well-worn clothes. Her hair, adorned with wood-shavings, was tied back from her face. Instead of being soft and manicured as most young women, her hands were calloused and stained.

'I'm sorry,' I muttered, tearing my eyes from her beautiful face. 'I've come to make full payment for the work he did.' I lowered my eyes. 'I was greedy and took advantage of his generosity, but I've found a better way.' I placed the proceeds from the sale of all four tables on their bench. 'Please forgive me.'

'You've met the Teacher, haven't you?' asked the young woman, reaching for a head scarf.

'How do you know?' I frowned.

She sniggered. 'Only Jesus could turn a pompous, self-centred man into a repentant one.'

'Deborah!' her mother scolded. She turned to me, fear in her eyes. 'I'm so sorry. Please forgive her.'

'She's right,' I whispered, not game to look at anyone in the room. 'I was self-centred and arrogant and greedy. I'm trying to change.'

Deborah dropped her half-tied scarf. 'You really did meet Him!'

I looked up, not prepared for the softness in her eyes. 'This morning,' I whispered. 'It's been the most amazing, confronting day of my life.' Quite why I was sharing this with total strangers I had no idea. A thought struck me then. 'Who is doing the work in the shop, if your father can't?'

'We're managing,' one of the young men answered.

I nodded, recognising the family pride hovering in the room.

'Would you stay for a meal?' Deborah asked. I saw the shock on her mother's face and saw her eyes track to the pot of lentils.

'My mother is expecting me tonight.' I stretched the truth.

'Perhaps tomorrow then?' one of the boys added. 'I'm sure Abba would have liked to break bread with you.'

'Thank you,' I answered, knowing that would give them time to buy and prepare a meal that was not an embarrassment. 'I look forward to tomorrow.' I caught the twinkle of fun and mischief in Deborah's eye.

So began my journey of selling my goods and giving money to the poor. And so began my journey of getting to know Deborah.

The Lesson

Leprosy! I wouldn't wish it on my worst enemy. Despair, degradation, disillusionment and pain lived amongst us… visiting without invitation… descending without warning.

Every day was the same. The sun rose. The sun set. In between, fevers rose. Frustration rose. Anger rose. Despair rose. Some nights the camp was quiet. Often it was filled with weeping and nightmares and arguments.

When I arrived, I thought I'd died and gone to the pit of hell. Disfigured men staggered around — if they could walk — in clothes, or rather rags, that hung on their skin-covered bones. Strips of cloth hung like funeral bandages, draped over oozing, smelly sores. Eyes, those not draped in dirty bandages, stared empty. There was no word besides empty — except dead.

I was met by a welcome party of walking dead. My pack snatched, my food stolen, my spare robe stolen. I couldn't blame them and, in the back of my mind, I wondered how long it would be before I became them. My whole being cried for what these men had lost. How many of them would have accosted a stranger and stolen his livelihood, before they were struck with leprosy? Despair does stupid things to a man.

I stood dazed, watching the men disappear over the ridge, still fighting over my bag of possessions. I gazed around, defeated. My shoulders dropped. My head dropped. My hope disappeared. Under some acacia trees, a group of men, although in pain, despair and grief like the rest of us, sat around a scroll — *a scroll* — really? Out here?

I stared.

They called me over. My heart smiled.

Life churned from one day to the next. Some mornings, baskets of food appeared on the other side of the palm grove — the invisible fence, the invisible barrier to freedom. Freedom that teased us through the palms where village rooftops glistened in the summer haze and children's laughter floated like a long-lost dream. Some days, I sat under the palms remembering or trying to remember my life before this hell-hole swallowed it.

One morning, a familiar voice wafted through the trees. *Deborah?* I stumbled towards the song floating up the hill.

A gravelly voice stopped me in my tracks. 'And what's a beautiful thing like you doing out here alone?' Anger burned in my middle. I stumbled faster to see an unshaven man leering at my daughter. His beard was unkempt, his grubby, brown tunic askew.

'Don't touch me!' she snarled. Deborah had not become any less defiant in the last two years.

'Or what?'

'Or I'll touch you!' I threatened, waving my dirty bandaged arm.

The man started.

'So will I,' a well-dressed man added. He puffed closer and dropped a bundle on the ground. Even from a distance, I could determine the expensive cut of his mantle and the careful sculpture of his beard.

'As will I,' called another staggering up the hill, baskets full of packages in each hand.

'No closer, Deborah!' I shouted, glaring as the leering man reddened and slunk away. 'What are you doing here, Bubbeleh?'

Her face collapsed. Her beautiful brown eyes filled. Tears danced on her lashes. 'Abba!'

By this time the basket-laden man had puffed his way to her side. Maybe I'd been here too long, but I was sure these were the men who had commissioned the carved tables in my past life... a hundred years ago, when I was healthy... when I was happy.

My visitors sat on the grass. They seemed comfortable together. Secret smiles. Silly giggles. It was obvious I had missed a great deal. The one I remembered as the servant opened his basket, shared a loaf and walked towards me. He left the basket where I could retrieve it. Bread, dates, olives and... letters. I clutched the letters to my chest, my eyes too blurred to read.

'Abba,' Deborah began. 'This is John Mark.' A strange look passed between them. 'And his servant Uzziah.'

I nodded. 'I recognise you. I made some carved tables for you.'

'Yes,' whispered John Mark. 'And I underpaid you. I was greedy and arrogant. I've made restitution to your family.' He held my gaze. Remorse filled his eyes. 'I ask your forgiveness too.'

'Apology accepted,' I nodded. 'I remember they were some of the most rewarding things I have ever made. And some of the most beautiful. But why the change of heart?'

John Mark took a deep breath and stared across the chasm between us. 'I met a man,' he answered.

'The Teacher?'

'You've heard of Him? Out here?'

I nodded. 'One of the men has a scroll. I don't understand how or why, but he showed us prophesies.' I picked at the corner of my tattered tunic. 'This Teacher …' I swallowed, not really sure if I should go on.

'Abba?'

I blew out my cheeks. 'This Teacher... seems to be the Messiah. Everything points to it. His birth, His family line... We've heard He does miracles,' I finished in a whisper.

'Miracles?' Deborah repeated.

Uzziah cleared his throat. 'They're right... and yes, He does miracles. I've seen Him heal a man with a withered hand and a boy with a spirit that threw him into the fire.'

Deborah stared at Uzziah, then at my bandages.

'We have to find Him first,' Uzziah sighed.

A commotion arose from the village below. Deborah jumped to her feet. 'I wonder what's happening.'

'We'd best go and see,' answered John Mark. 'Enjoy your basket of food, Sir.'

Deborah held her hands towards me. 'Oh Abba, I so want to hug you.'

My eyes filled as I waved them down the short slope to the road where a crowd of people, laughing and singing, engulfed them. Behind me, I sensed men pressing in. In a glance I realised they were the ones who read the scrolls with me. They stopped behind me.

'Do you think it's Him?' one whispered, clutching his dirty bandaged arm to his chest.

I glanced back to the crowd on the road. One man stood out. How, I have no idea. He was dressed the same, beard the same, skin the same, but somehow He was different.

'It *is* Him,' another announced, running... staggering down the slope. His tunic, dirty and torn barely covered the sores on his legs.

Others followed. I gasped when they crossed the exclusion barrier, but joined them anyway, stuffing my precious letters into my tunic.

'Jesus of Nazareth!' one called. 'Have mercy on us!'

The crowd pulled back. One lady screamed.

Jesus stepped closer — towards us! 'Remove your bandages,' He ordered. 'Andrew,' He called to one of His men, 'make a fire and burn them.'

Remove our bandages? Burn them? Then I saw the glint of a smile in the Teacher's eye. I ripped off my bandages and gasped. Not a sore, not a spot, not a blemish, not a scar, marred my skin.

'Now,' called the Teacher, pointing further down the hill, 'Go down and bathe in the stream, then show yourselves to the priest.'

The joyous cries and sobbing laughter of my nine outcast friends echoed down to the stream and back along the road towards the village.

I stood in front of the Teacher and fell to my knees. 'Thank You,' I wept. 'I know You are Jesus, the Lord, the Messiah. Yet You had mercy on me, a Samaritan.' I fell on my face.

A strong hand pulled me to my feet. Deep brown eyes pierced mine and held my gaze. Then without warning I was wrapped in warm powerful arms. My eyes ran, my nose ran. I knew I smelt, but it didn't seem to worry Him. The first touch in two years, that embrace empowered me.

'Now,' Jesus whispered in my ear. 'Go and wash in the stream and show yourself to the priest.'

I watched John Mark step forward. The two men clasped forearms. They locked eyes, nodded and smiled.

'Come on, Abba,' Deborah called. 'You really need that stream.'

'Stay there, Bubbeleh. I think the men would be more comfortable without you.'

Uzziah chuckled and held out a fresh tunic.

A fresh tunic! Clean clothes! My heart wept for the poor leprous men left behind — those who didn't follow us — those who will spend the rest of their lives in pain and exclusion. I resolved then and there to somehow make life a little kinder for them.

How, I had no idea, but I'd met the God of miracles!

Based on Mark 10:17–27
Matthew 19:16–22
Luke 17:11–19

Salome

I guess everyone wishes for things
they don't have.
Can't have.
Will never have.
Some wish for palaces and banquets.
Some for fame and fortune.
I wish for freedom.
Freedom to run barefoot in the dirt.
Freedom to whisper silly secrets
and giggle with friends.
Freedom from palaces and banquets.
Freedom from fame and fortune and gold
And expectations and dirty secrets.

Most of all,
I wish for a mother who cares for me.
Loving arms to hold me,
And Peace.

Salome

I HATE MY LIFE.

Fine linen curtains, dyed blue and red, tied with exquisite golden chains, hang over my window. Mosaic tiles depicting a country scene in colourful patterns and swirls lie under an ugly, expensive rug I detest. I'd rather see the beautiful tiles — the country, the trees, the grass — freedom.

Joanna, my elderly nursemaid, is my only real friend and she's not supposed to be a friend. So, I'm stuck here in my gilded cage, watching the world go by. Watching young children run up the dusty road with liberty I'll never have. Watching the village girls, dressed in simple tunics and shawls and sandals, skip under my window, arm in arm, giggling with secrets I can never share.

But I have my own secrets — as hateful as they are. I know what my mother is up to. I know the dirty secrets of the palace. I know what she and Herod are planning.

How I wish I could live with my father. Life would be so wonderful, so free, away from the palace scrutiny and cold stares. But it is deemed a girl needs her mother to teach her the social graces and poise of one in my station.

My station! My station is as fragile as the next spear thrust and I need my mother's influence like a bucket of slime from the cesspit.

Does she not think anyone can see her flirting? Does she not think anyone knows her plans — plans for power and wealth? Does she not think of anyone else? My father's grief … my grief. No, of course not! As far as my mother is concerned, she's the only one who matters. Watching her openly seduce Herod broke my father and revolts me. No, I don't need her influence.

My window seat is my private, secret place. I pull the curtain across and retreat, wishing my life to be as simple and carefree as the children playing below. Wishing for love. I know father loves me, but he's leagues away. Joanna's arms are the only ones to mother me. I remember sitting on her lap, listening to the stories of her people. Oh, how wonderful it was. I'm too big for that now, but I have a sudden urge to hear those stories again. I tip my head against the window-frame, watching the gathering dusk take the children home.

'Salome!' My mother's voice sounds like a peacock screech. 'Salome!'

I whisper goodnight to the children and jump from my hidden ledge just in time to hear my door bang open. 'Where are you, girl? You should be at your dance lesson.'

Dance lessons! Another social grace I must endure. Although, to be truthful, dancing gives me a freedom I enjoy. To twirl is freedom. To jump is power. To leap is supremacy. I can let my thoughts go and let my body take over. It's really the only thing she cannot control.

She can, however, control the costumes, the gold head-piece, the flimsy scarfs, the uncomfortable ankle chains. I endure them only so I can dance. I pound out my frustration with routine moves, with leaps and spins. It's exhilarating but exhausting.

I plead fatigue at dinner time and request my meal to be served in my rooms. Another night of watching the flirting and fawning and giggling? — no way. Mother even ordered his and her identical cushions for the dinner recliners. How the slaves can keep a straight face is beyond me.

I make sure Joanna joins me for the evening meal. I need a hug and a story. We eat together. My mother would have a fit if she knew.

When I request a story, Joanna beams. She brushes my hair and begins. 'Wise men came from the east, asking Herod — Herod the Great, that is, your grandfather — where the new king had been born. They had seen His star and had come to worship him.'

'I bet Grandpa Herod was not pleased with that!' I scoffed, trying to imagine Herod Antipas' reaction — let alone my mother's.

'You're right, Bubbeleh. However, he called his scholars together to find what the Scriptures said. They determined Bethlehem was where the king of the Jews was to be born.'

'It's in the Scriptures? There was a king besides Caesar?'

Joanna pats my cheek. I lean into the gentleness of her hand. She looks into the distance and smiles. *'But you, Bethlehem, in the land of Judah, are not the least among the rulers of Judah. For out of you shall come a Ruler who will shepherd My people, Israel.'*

'Wasn't Herod angry?'

'Oh, yes. He was angry, but it seems he held himself together. He told the wise men to come back to see him so he could go and worship the king too.'

I could feel my excitement growing. 'Really? So, did the wise men find a king?'

Joanna chuckles. 'Yes, but an angel told them to go home a different way.'

'An angel?' I jump to my knees. 'A real angel?'

Joanna nods. 'Herod was actually wanting to kill the baby king.'

'Kill a baby?' I stare at Joanna in disbelief.

She sighs. Her eyes fill with tears.

'What's wrong, Joanna? What happened? Didn't the king get away?'

She plays with the hem of her tunic. 'Herod ordered all the baby boys under two years old to be killed.'

Horror hits me in the gut with an ice-cold thud. I am unable to speak, unable to think, unable to breathe.

In that moment, I loathe my family and all they — we — stand for, arrogance, greed, pride. Am I like that?

Joanna drops her head into her hands and weeps.

I have never seen her cry like this before and don't quite know what to do, so I sit like a statue. Then it dawns upon me. I know nothing about Joanna's family or her life before coming to the palace. I always figured she was here to look after me. Maybe I'm more like my mother than I realise — I hope not.

'Joanna,' I whisper. 'You had a baby boy too?'

She closes her eyes.

'And the baby king was killed too,' I mutter. 'God's plans were ruined by Herod.'

Joanna wipes her eyes. 'No,' she whispers.

'He got away?'

Joanna smiles through her glassy eyes and nods. 'An angel told His parents to flee to Egypt. They stayed there until Herod the Great died. Then they came back to Israel and settled in Galilee. Now He's a grown man and travels the land preaching and healing the sick.'

I frown, confused. 'How do you know? I thought you said He was a king.'

Joanna smiles. 'I've met Him,' she whispers.

I stare in disbelief. 'You've met a king besides Caesar?'

'Oh, Bubbeleh, He is so wise.' She glances around the room and leans close to me, still whispering. 'His kingdom is not of this world. His teachings are of peace and love. I wish you could meet Him. Herod has imprisoned His friend, John, who is called the Baptiser.'

'I've heard of him. Mother says he's evil,' I whisper back. Quite why our conversation has become hushed, I'm not sure. But Joanna continues to whisper too.

'No, my Bubbeleh, John is not evil. He's full of God's spirit. He did, however, tell Herod it was not lawful for him to have your mother as she is his brother's wife.'

'So that's it... Mother again.'

My prison sentence continues, day by day, week by week. I watch the children, covet the life of the giggling girls and wish my mother loved me. Dance is my release.

Herod's impending birthday brings a hive of activity to the palace — new curtains, new cloths, new cushions, new clothes and swarms of summer flies. My mother tells me I'm to dance — a gift for the king. Looks like I'm the gift, but I get to practice dance all day. I wonder if the giggling girls miss me? I miss them.

A celebration dinner to eclipse all celebration dinners will be attended by anyone who is anyone. And I have to dance in front of them all. I pull my costume up, trying to cover more of my chest. I wipe my hands down the sides of my flimsy skirt, only to catch my palm on a gold sequin. I flinch. My hand is bleeding. I suck it, willing it to heal. I smile. Maybe I need Joanna's king to heal me.

The music starts.

My soul stirs.

The drums empower me, taking me to a place of freedom. I dance. No one else is in the room. It's just me. My mind escapes. My body is set free with only drums and music to obey. All too soon, it's over and I return to my captivity. I kneel before Herod ... a panting, sweaty, hate-filled twelve-year-old.

He stands and claps. I glance at my mother. She's smiling — *smiling?* Herod sits and tips my chin up. His beady eyes meet mine. 'Whatever you ask for I will give you, up to half my kingdom.'

I hear gasps and whispers. Out of the corner of my eye, I see my mother beckon me. I bow to Herod. He laughs. 'Go talk to your mother, my daughter.'

Daughter? He may as well have covered me in slime.

Mother's eyes glint in triumph. Her mouth smirks in glee. 'Ask for the head of John the Baptiser on a silver platter.'

My hands fly to my face. 'What?' I gasp.

'You heard me.' Mother's voice is low and threatening.

I stare in horror.

She raises her right eyebrow. That look says, 'It's him or you.'

I lurch back and bump into one of the guests, a fat old man whose look says more than I am capable of comprehending. He is drunk and his hands are undisciplined.

Mother's eyes bore into my soul and, at that moment, I know she is capable of anything. I am nothing but her ticket to power.

I stagger back to Herod and stand defiant. 'I wish the head of John the Baptiser on a wooden platter.' Mother had asked for a silver platter. *Sorry, mother, I may not have won this round, but I didn't lose it either.*

I am not prepared for Herod's reaction. He slumps into his chair, closes his eyes and raises his hand. Guards leave. Music starts. I stumble into a corner, collapse behind a curtain and clasp my hands over the back of my neck wishing I could melt and become part of the curtain. No — then I'd have to stay and watch my mother's displays. I want to run. I want to hide. How long I sat and trembled I have no idea, but it felt like an eternity. It wasn't nearly long enough.

An old glassy-eyed servant finds me. 'My lady, the guards are searching for you.'

I frown.

'The head is ready.'

Based on Matthew 14:6-11

A Basket of Figs

God is all powerful
Majestic,
Holy,
Pure,
Omnipotent,
All knowing ...
But I have learnt He still needs
Your hands ... my hands,
Your feet ... my feet,
Your love ... my love,
To accomplish His will here on earth.
So, help one another, serve one another,
forgive one another,
That His love can flow and in His name
be glorified.

A Basket of Figs

DRIZZLE WASHES OUT this morning's dawn. Hopefully it'll be clear by this afternoon, so our little gang can hunt for figs.

Meanwhile, morning studies wait as usual. Our teacher's name is Rabbi Samson. I bet he copped a lot when he was growing up. But I guess he could actually say his name. I was six before I could pronounce Zedekiah, so, I'm just Zed.

Today's lessons are surprisingly interesting, but I'm happy once we're finished. Amma always has lunch ready when I get home. I gobble it down and head for the door. Amma holds me tight. I realise I'm nearly as tall as her. She brushes my dark hair out of my eyes. 'Have to trim this soon,' she says, 'or your kippah won't stay on.'

'Hadassa, let him be,' my father chuckles. 'He'll be tied down to society soon enough.' He eyes met me with a stern look. 'Have you done your chores, Zed?'

I grin. 'Yes, Abba.'

Amma kisses my forehead. 'Off you go then, but be careful.'

'Always, Amma,' I laugh, wiping my face as I run out the door.

The others are waiting when I puff to a halt. Josiah, as usual, is tying his sandals at the last minute, Joses, licking his fingers from lunch and Eliakim straightening his tunic.

'Let's go!' I call. We follow Josiah. At thirteen, he is the unofficial leader. Eliakim and I are not far behind. We both turn twelve next Passover and Joses is a year behind that, although he's just as tall as me. Ages don't really matter. We're friends and have been as long as we can remember. A ragtag team, relishing the freedom of early spring adventures.

'Good afternoon, boys,' a familiar voice calls.

'Afternoon, Rabbi Simeon,' I answer, waving. 'Would you like some more figs?'

We have two rabbis in our village. Rabbi Samson is our teacher and Rabbi Simeon is always out and about, encouraging people, helping people, meeting people, fixing things.

Sometimes rabbis from Jerusalem visit our village. Their long black robes drag in the dust, their tefillin tied tightly to their brows, their shawls seeming to sit suspended on their heads. Rabbi Simeon doesn't dress like that, except for synagogue. He strides over to us. 'No figs for me today.' His smile is dazzling. 'I still have some left, but I'm sure Widow Sarah would appreciate a basketful.'

Because of the rain, there are lots of delicious muddy puddles. Joses and I take off our sandals and jump in the biggest one. Mud splashes. We laugh. Josiah shakes his head. Eliakim steps around the puddle. I know it's so he doesn't get his tunic muddy. I also know he only has two, and the reason I know that is because they are two I grew out of. They were pretty worn by time I finished with them, but Amma mended them and sewed some extra fabric on the bottom. Josiah gave Eliakim a nicer tunic which he keeps for Synagogue best. Joses has three little brothers to hand his clothes down to.

Our afternoon follows the usual route. We race between the trinket stall and the leather shop where Abba works. That brings us right to the bakery. 'Afternoon, boys,' Thomas calls. 'I'm about to put some raisin buns in the oven.'

Joses laughs. 'We'll be sure to find some juicy figs then.'

Searching for extra juicy figs to trade for raisin buns is part of our ritual. We always manage to find some and Thomas is always ready — with his goofy surprised look.

We climb the rocks and scramble onto the village wall. 'Bit slippery here!' Josiah calls.

Some of the stones on the wall are wobbly, but that just makes it more fun and more adventurous. The jump to the ground is the second adventure and then we are free to run in the field. Next to the brook grows an ancient fig tree. It's loaded. Filling Eliakim's basket with firm figs is our first priority. His amma dries them to sell at the markets. Next, we search for some big juicy ones to trade for our usual raisin buns from Thomas' bakery. Then Joses, Josiah and I fill a bag to take home. Today we collect extra for Widow Sarah. My mouth waters. I can't wait any longer. Fig juice dribbles down my arms, my face, my tunic. I tip my head to the sky and groan in delight, noticing the other boys doing the same.

We leave our figs under the tree and explore the brook, making plans to fish one day when the weather warms up. We have to go the long way back because the wall is too high to scale on this side. Arms loaded with our haul and sticks in our spare hands, we are soldiers, protecting the village from bears and lions.

'Don't you dare come inside with those muddy feet!' Amma warns when I arrive home. How she sees me from the hearth, I'll never know.

'Never!' I grin, heading towards the well. I draw some water. It's freezing, but clean — clean before I deal with my feet, anyway. I can see why Amma insists on a separate bucket for drinking water. I slosh the mud off my feet, tip the water into the garden, rinse the bucket and grabbed an old towel. There's still mud up my legs. Bother. There's no way Amma will miss that. More cold water, more scrubbing, more water for the garden and my legs are tingling and clean enough to pass even Amma's scrutiny.

She chuckles. 'Good job, Zed. Now, run and ask Eliakim and Rachel if they'd like to come for dinner. Looks like I've made too much again.'

I laugh. We all know Amma's ploy. Eliakim's father died two years ago. A widow's life is not easy, but our village pulls together around Rachel and Eliakim. The men made a lean-to at the back of her house with wooden racks to dry figs and grapes. She sells these at the markets. However, her income isn't always steady and taxes need to be paid and food needs to be bought.

Rachel falls into Amma's arms when she arrives. They both weep. 'We're here to help,' Amma whispers. 'Remember, I've been where you are. If it wasn't for the help of a secret benefactor, Rhoda and I would probably not be here. I'd love to find out who it was.'

I don't know how my little sister, Rhoda, knows when someone needs a cuddle, but at three years old she can figure it out — just a gift, I guess. Amma was a widow with Rhoda just able to walk when Abba met her. They married a year later. He calls her 'Mama Bear', though I have no idea why.

I have another sister, Leah. She's fourteen and as far as sisters go, she's okay. She slips into the room and helps Rachel with her shawl. Our real amma died about six years ago. Now Hadassa is our amma and we love her.

Eliakim stands outside the door, looking at the ground. I grab his hand and pull him over the threshold.

'Thanks,' he whispers. 'I know my amma does her best, but I'm so tired of dried figs and barley bread for dinner.'

Today is Friday. We don't gather figs for Rachel on Fridays because she doesn't get time to finish preparing them before sunset when Sabbath begins. That doesn't stop our adventures. We still need to fill our stomachs and find figs to trade for our raisin buns.

We had more rain during the night. Puddles are everywhere, but for some reason, I don't feel like jumping in them today. I don't know why... it just feels wrong. None of us has the usual spring in our step today. Maybe it's the rain... but I feel it's more than that. Something's not right. Today, we just walk between the stalls, greet Thomas and climb the wall.

'Watch your step!' Josiah calls from in front. 'Some of the stones are loose.'

I follow, being careful to test each stone before putting my weight down. It makes it a bit challenging.

A clatter, a scream. I spin around. Eliakim tumbles down the wall behind me. Rocks tumble down after him. A loud crack and I know he has broken something. My heart stops, then takes off with a jolt.

'Eliakim!' Josiah screams, jumping down. 'Zed! Get your Abba!'

I gasp, staring at my friend. His leg sticks out from his body at a strange angle. There's blood.

'Zed!' Josiah screams again.

I turn and scramble back along the wall, past wide-eyed Joses. My legs pound. My heart pounds. My throat screams. Abba grabs me and holds me tight. 'Eliakim,' I gasp, 'fell off the wall... broke his leg.' Abba calls some men. I have no idea how many. My head is spinning. I tumble back after them, gathering Joses on the way.

The jump from the wall we thought was the bravest thing in our adventures is only as high as my father's broad chest. He pokes his head over the top. 'Zed, tell Doctor Luke to meet us at Rachel's.'

'Doctor?' I gasp.

Abba meets my eyes and nods.

I grab Joses and take off, willing my lungs to catch enough air for a breath. If Abba thinks Eliakim needs a doctor, it must be bad. My lungs are still gasping when the men arrive with Abba carrying Eliakim close to his chest. I see Abba catch Amma's eye as Rachel falls into her arms. He shakes his head. What does that mean?

I don't know when Joses left.

I pace.

I wring my hands.

I sit.

I stand.

Eliakim screams.

Rhoda cuddles my leg. I lift her onto my knee and bury my face into her dark curls and sob.

Evening is approaching, which means Sabbath is approaching. I call Leah, guessing it's time to prepare for dinner. No answer. Searching the house doesn't reveal anything. Then I hear a sob coming from Rachel's drying room.

'Leah?'

Leah sniffs. 'If we don't get these figs finished tonight, they'll be wasted.'

'What do you need me to do?'

'First, wash your hands in that bowl.' Leah almost smiles. 'Gather up the figs that are dry and put them in this basket. They need one of those little pieces of cloth between layers.'

How does Leah know this stuff? I don't argue. There are rows and rows to collect.

A shadow blocks the light. 'Time to come inside,' Abba announces from the doorway, taking a glance at the sky. 'It's Sabbath and God's Word says we mustn't work on His day.'

I look at the basket of figs waiting to be sliced and sigh. *What a waste.*

Leah stands tall. 'Yes, Abba, but God also says to look after the widows and orphans.'

Abba closes his eyes and nods.

'Abba?' Leah whispers. 'Could you close the canvas flyover? The dew rots the figs.'

He nods. He doesn't even have to stand on tippy-toe to pull the roof across. 'What can I do to help?'

I stare in wonder, but Leah just orders him around like she orders me. 'Help Zed gather up the figs that are dry. Be careful, only get the dry ones or they'll go mouldy. Zed, let Abba finish that. You go through the basket and pick out any squished ones. We'll preserve them. These are the figs you gathered on Thursday morning and they've been sitting here for almost two days.'

While Leah is ordering us around, her hands, with a mind of their own, are slicing a new batch. She glances into the dusk and up at Abba. He smiles.

With the newly sliced figs spread onto the racks and the canvas sides drawn over the drying room, Abba picks up the basket of preserve-destined figs.

Just one more job for me. One I love. Time to set the mouse traps. 'Come on, puss.' Eliakim's cat strolls in. He's big and white and has one eye. We call him 'Solomon'. My cat follows. Black as night. We wanted to call her 'Jezebel', but Rachel wouldn't let us... so, she's just 'Blacky'... boring, I know, but she doesn't seem to mind.

Our house is sombre. Amma's eyes are glassy and red. She sits on a chair holding Rhoda who is patting her cheek. Flatbread and fig jam, lentil soup and herbs are spread on the table.

Next to the water jug, I spy five raisin buns. 'Thomas?'

Amma tries to smile.

All night I toss and turn.

All night I pray.

All night I try to figure how I could have stopped Eliakim falling.

Even though it's the Sabbath, Abba lets me go to see Eliakim. It's only next door so it's not considered a journey. I'm not prepared for what I see. Eliakim is as pale as the sheets he's lying on. His dark hair is matted. Pain contorts his face. Dried blood mars his arm. But it's the state of his leg that frightens me. Two pieces of wood tied top and bottom and at his knee straddle his leg. Blood still seeps from a gash on his thigh between them. Doctor Luke picks up a bowl of bloody cloths. 'Looks like you have a visitor,' he whispers to Eliakim.

'I can come back later if it'd be better,' I stammer, desperate to stay.

'A visitor would be the best tonic I can think of,' the doctor smiles. 'He might be a bit drowsy though. I've just given him some herbs.'

Eliakim groans, 'Zed,' and closes his eyes. He tries to open them again, but just succeeds in raising his eyebrows. 'Talk to me.'

I tell him about preparing the figs in the drying room and how Abba stayed to help even after sunset. Eliakim opens one eye at that bit of news. A twitch of a grin crosses his mouth. I tell him Thomas delivered raisin buns to our house and that the rain has stopped. But most of all I just sit with him and watch him sleep… doze, really. I can see spams of pain cross his face.

I go the next day and the next. Sometimes I talk about all our adventures. Sometimes I tell him about the things Samson is teaching. I figure he'll need to know them for when we celebrate our Bar Mitzvah next year. Sometimes I just sit, but I'm sure he knows I'm there. When Doctor Luke comes to bathe his leg, I leave. It doesn't seem to be getting any better.

On Wednesday, Amma hands me a covered pot to take over. 'Broth,' she says. 'Doctor Luke thinks he might be well enough to sip some.'

My heart soars. Eliakim is getting better.

When I enter Eliakim's room, I nearly lose my breakfast. *The smell!* Clutching the jar like a lifeline, I swallow and stare in desperation at Rabbi Simeon who is standing near the window. He closes his eyes and tips his head, indicating for me to follow. We slump onto a bench by the hearth … me, still holding the pot of broth, Rabbi Simeon, grim-faced, Rachel, staring with eyes empty, full of desperation and defeat. Black circles drag at her face. I will not believe what I see. I put the broth on the table, pull my tunic over my nose, walk to Eliakim's room and tell him I'll see him tomorrow. Rachel hugs me.

Somehow, I sit through Rabbi Samson's lessons. Joses and Josiah wear the same fear, the same pain as I do. I think Rabbi Samson feels sorry for us because lessons are short today. I shuffle home knowing it's lunchtime, but today, I'm not hungry.

At the door, I stand frozen to the spot, looking at the little neckline Amma is stitching, looking at the billowing white linen sitting at her feet like clouds, looking at my best friend's funeral shroud.

'Eliakim's going to die?' I whisper.

Mama drops her stitching and holds her arms towards me.

'No!' I hear myself scream.

I run, blinded by fear, blinded by anger and confusion.

I run.

I don't know which direction I am going. I just run. I have to get away.

I bump into someone. I don't care.

I splash through a puddle. I don't care.

I run.

Wild rage courses through me… my legs fuelled by a fierceness that frightens me.

Someone calls my name. I don't care.

I run into something.

It's a bear! Huge arms enfold me. I hear my name.

I kick. I scream. I bite. The bear's arms tighten.

Something in the back of my mind reminds me to play dead if a bear attacks. I go limp. The bear lifts me off my feet.

So, this is how I'm going to die. I take my last breath. It doesn't smell like a bear.

I open my eyes. *Why is a bear wearing a coat?*

I hear my name again — louder this time — clearer.

Rabbi Simeon! He lifts me higher and carries me through a sea of babbling voices. 'Move aside,' he commands. 'He'll be fine.'

Who'll be fine? I hope he's not talking about me. *I'll never be fine. Eliakim is going to die.* A scream burns my throat. Simeon holds me close. I can feel his steps quicken. I hear a door slam. I'm lowered onto a stool.

'Zed,' Simeon begins.

'You lied to me,' I seethe. 'You lied.' I jump up. 'You all lied!'

Rabbi Simeon starts. *Good!* Let him feel guilty.

'That's quite a serious accusation, Zed,' Rabbi Simeon replies.

I point my finger at him. 'You said God was loving. You said He cared. You said everything is for His glory.' My throat closes. I take a deep breath. 'What sort of God needs a little boy to die for His glory?'

Simeon reaches for my hand. I pull away.

'Amma is making Eliakim's funeral clothes,' I whisper. 'He's going to die.' I drop onto the stool. 'My best friend is going to die.'

Rabbi Simeon raises his tear-filled eyes to me. 'Zed, God didn't push Eliakim off the wall. The stones were loose and slippery. He fell and broke his leg.'

'Other people have had broken bones,' I answer.

Rabbi Simeon takes a deep breath. 'Zed, Eliakim's bone was poking through his skin.'

I stare back at this horrible thought.

'His blood got poisoned from the dirt. That's why he got the fever. His body can't fight it. The poison is eating his leg.'

My eyes narrow. 'Where's God's love then?'

'Maybe you're God's love.'

Is he mad?

Rabbi Simeon paused. 'Maybe giving Eliakim such a good friend as you to help him through all this is God's love. You've been there every day, Zed, talking to him, giving him hope. Even this morning, when the smell of his rotting leg was so bad, you were there with unconditional love.'

'Rabbi Simeon, Eliakim is going to die! What use was it?'

It happens during the night. Empty eyes greet me in the morning. Abba stays home. Leah sobs. Amma raises red, tear-filled eyes. Rhoda runs towards me. I pick her up. She clutches me tight.

Abba steers me to the table. 'It's going to be a long road ahead, Son,' he murmurs, putting a raisin bun into my hand. I frown. 'Thomas just wanted to let you know he's thinking of you. Don't let his gift go to waste. I believe the other boys got one too.'

Tears dribbled down my face as I pick a raisin out. Eliakim didn't get one. I break my bun in half and share it with Rhoda, determined to stand strong for Eliakim.

The day drags on. I cry. I determine again to be strong. I fail. I cry. I venture outside but can't stand the sympathetic stares and nods from the people who are paying their respects. Slumping at the table, my gaze tracks to Leah. 'Do we need to turn the figs again today?'

It's almost a look of relief that crosses Leah's face. 'At least we'll be doing something,' she mutters, swiping her cheek.

Solomon and Blacky have been busy. Three dead mice sit on the doorstep. 'I wonder how many they ate?' I almost smile.

The roof is open to the sunlight. The dried figs we so carefully collected on the Sabbath are gone. Coins sit in the empty basket. Another basket of dried fruit sits ready to sell — the ones we cut and spread 'that' evening. More surprisingly, the racks are full and a third basket overflowing with choice fruit sits on the workbench. Leah frowns. 'Abba must have already been here.'

I raise the cloth to discover five raisin buns. 'It wasn't Abba.'

Keeping our hands busy helps calm our minds and eats the time away. We talk — more than we've ever done before. I tell her of our ritual route to collect the figs, of our trade with Thomas, of our plans to fish in the brook next spring. She tells me of the hours she spends with Rachel learning to dry fruit and her deep desire to study the Scriptures. Leah can read and write better than most boys in the village. She also knows her numbers. Abba taught us both. We sit on the floor in the drying room long after the figs are cut and laid out. It seems a good place to be and we're not in any hurry to face the next thing — Eliakim's funeral.

Eliakim's funeral procession is the worst thing I have ever been to. Although a beautiful outpouring of love from the villagers, it's also a dreadful outpouring of grief. No one wears coloured clothes. All heads are covered. Eyes are downcast and faces stony.

Amma holds one hand tight and, to my surprise, Leah holds my other hand. We walk directly in front of the men carrying the bier. Behind us, Abba and Thomas walk with Rachel — holding her up really.

In an instant, Amma stops. The procession stops too, as if from an unsaid command. *What is happening?* Rhoda tears away from the woman holding her and clings to a strange man's legs. Amma darts forward and falls at his feet. 'Please, Rabbi,' she sobs. 'He's all she has.'

Rabbi? He doesn't look like a rabbi.

The man raises Amma to her feet and steps towards Eliakim. I can see tears in his eyes. The crowd steps back. He and touches Rachel's cheek and looks to the sky. I look up too but there's nothing there.

Wait… was that a flash of light?

The stranger's voice re-focuses me. 'Eliakim, wake up.' He reaches out and touches Eliakim's cold, white face.

I wanted to scream at him and tell him Eliakim was dead, not asleep. Everyone here could have told him, but the man says it again.

Rachel's wail startles everyone. She surges forward, leaping out of Thomas' arms.

'Amma!' whispers a familiar voice.

What?

Eliakim sits up. He sits up! He turns and swings his legs, one by one, over the side of the bier. Even through the shroud, I can see they're whole. His legs are whole.

Rachel screams, frozen to the spot. The man takes her hand and leads her to the bier.

'Amma,' Eliakim whispers again, reaching out. She holds him, sobbing. We're all sobbing. Thomas lifts Eliakim from the bier. Gasps, sobs, wails, laughter explode all around. Rachel turns to the stranger and falls at his feet just like Amma did. Eliakim joins her.

With strong arms, the stranger pulls them both up.

'I know who You are,' Eliakim whispers, hugging the man fiercely around the waist.

'Shh,' the stranger answers. 'We'll talk later.'

From somewhere in front of the procession, Rabbi Simeon strides over and hugs the man, thumping him in the back. 'Jesus!'

Rabbi Samson looks over and raises his eyebrows in question. Simeon nods.

Jesus?

Someone takes the bier away. Someone sets up tables right there in the street. Someone brings benches and stools. Someone — it could be the same someone, I have no idea — loads the tables with wooden plates piled high with food.

Waving His hand towards the feast, Jesus says, 'Looks like it's time to celebrate.'

Rachel lowers her head. 'I can't join in. I've touched a dead body.'

Jesus looks around. 'I don't see any dead body around here. Did you, Rabbi Simeon?'

'Not one,' Rabbi Simeon smiles. 'How about you, Rabbi Samson?'

'I believe Jesus said the boy was sleeping,' Rabbi Samson answers. 'He seems to be awake now.'

Eliakim laughs. 'I'm starved! Come on, Zed, let's eat.'

I still haven't moved. Leah still holds my hand. I don't think I've taken a single breath in the last five minutes. Eliakim pulls my other hand. 'Come on.'

'Wait,' Rachel calls. 'Maybe you should get changed first.'

'No, Amma,' Eliakim answers. 'I want to remember today. I want everyone to remember today. I want everyone to see my shroud and give praise to God.'

Rachel nods. 'Maybe you could get a belt, then. That gown is so long, you could fall and break…' She gasps.

I give Eliakim my belt and together we hoist up the billowing fabric, turning him into a walking cloud. Jesus laughs. With Josiah and Joses, we grab a plate. Everyone stands back. So many mixed emotions swirl around us, but for once we get first pick at the food, even though we're just boys. But I guess — Eliakim is the guest of honour.

I watch Jesus. I watch my parents and Rachel and Thomas and the rabbis laugh and eat as though they are old friends. I watch Rhoda in Jesus' arms. I hear Him call Amma 'Mama Bear' and watch her blush.

Eliakim drags me over and grabs Jesus' hand. 'We're celebrating our Bar Mitzvah next Passover,' he says. 'Would You like to come?'

As strange look passes over Jesus' face. He cups our chins. 'I'd like that very much,' He whispers. 'But My Father has a job for Me to do in Jerusalem next Passover.'

Based on Luke 7:11–17

It Could Have Been Me

Murder was nothing new to me.
I took lives.
I granted pardon.

I was the King of the Underworld.
Death comes to us all in this miserable land
overrun with unclean invaders.
Romans.
How I hate them.
This man, though, I swear was different.
His death, senseless, brutal.

I've seen many men die but none so gracious,
so calm, so… powerful.
I couldn't turn away.
Something happened to me there at the foot
of His cross.

It Could Have Been Me

ROUGH ROMAN HANDS throw me into the crowd. Someone spits. Someone punches. Smelly arms haul me to my feet and carry me away — though the crowd, through the jeers, through the manic screams. The mob is out for blood — for once it isn't mine

'Crucify Him!' The cries follow us, echoing on the stones, on the buildings… through my head.

Toothless mouths grin. Congratulations flow. Hands slap my back. My men crowd around. Dancing and whooping erupt on all sides. 'We sure showed 'em, Boss!'

I knew my men would stand by me, but I must admit, this is the closest call I have ever had. To tell the truth, I have never been so scared. My hands ball into fists at the thought of the cross… the nails… the pain.

It could be me.

I let myself be led through the back streets of Jerusalem away from the mob, away from the noise — a smile is plastered on my face. I wonder how many of them know what a fake smile it is. Jonas would have known. I swallow. Jonas is no longer here. He had become too friendly with a certain lady and ended up on the wrong end of a Roman sword.

That's one of the problems with our line of work. Murder and thievery is a dangerous sport — if you get caught, that is. Otherwise, it's a lucrative adventure.

'Crucify Him! Crucify Him!' the echoes chase us… buffet us down the street. They tear at my gut. I stumble.

Strong arms grab me. 'Hey, Boss, you been in prison too long.' Guffaws wash over me.

Fake smile. Fake smile. Let them celebrate.

Murderous cries swirl down the street. 'Crucify Him! Crucify Him!'

My heart bounces in my chest like a bucking mule. I've been in some pretty tricky situations in my life, but that was the worst.

It was Him or me.

If He ever had been human, He isn't now. His face is swollen to twice its size. Blood seeps from where they tore His beard out. Blood leaks over His face. I have no idea why they rammed that crown of thorns on His head. That's beyond torture. His clothes — what's left of them — are torn and bloodied, although they saved His tunic… said it was valuable.

Everything else is a mess — except His eyes.

They had looked straight at me — through me — into my soul. No condemnation, no contempt, no criticism — just… I'm not really sure what. I want to say 'love', but that's impossible. How could there be love in the eyes of someone who is about to die a torturous death?

As if He hasn't suffered enough already! I heard the lashes. I counted them. Thirty-nine — and He's still alive — barely, but He's alive.

I've killed many men. I've roughed up more than I can remember, but never have I seen a human in such a state. I keep telling myself He's just a man. But I'm not sure that's true… Of course it's true!

He bled. He cried out. He stumbled. He fell… He looked at me with those pure, pure eyes.

My gut clenches again.

I have to go back.

My men keep jostling me, pushing me, laughing, rejoicing, congratulating each other.

Fake smile. Fake smile.

I have to go back.

With strength I didn't know I could still muster, and a roar from my inner gut, I reef my arms from my men's triumphant hands. My lungs heave. My head pounds. My men freeze, silent, dumfounded.

'Barabbas?' Reuben steps forward, powerful arms spread. 'Barabbas?'

I hold his gaze. 'I have to go back.'

Behind Reuben, my men slink into the shadows like the rats they are.

'Are you crazy?' Reuben gasps. 'That mob's mad. They're out for blood. They'll grab you too.'

I close my eyes. Jesus' gaze still burns through my soul. 'I have to go back.'

I take a step back, my eyes fixed on Reuben. Another step back and another, and another, then I stumble and fall… sprawled on my back. Rocks slice into the scabbed wounds from the lashes. My head swims. Reuben holds my stare but doesn't offer a hand up. This is the leadership challenge he's been working towards. I lie spreadeagled, waiting for his knife. I have avoided death once today. My luck can't hold any longer.

Reuben just looks at me. Confusion? Pity? Contempt? He shakes his head, turns and rejoins the men. His broad back is the last thing I see as they enter the shadows.

Scabs open on my elbows, and knees, adding their pain to my bleeding, gouged shoulder. I scramble up and stumble… towards the wild, blood-thirsty mob.

'Crucify Him! Crucify Him!'

Pulling my shawl over my head, I creep around the last corner. The Roman soldiers are everywhere — more than I can ever remember seeing in one place. How I hate the Romans! Pontius Pilate is speaking. I strain to hear what he's saying. He's washing his hands.

Typical!

Don't get involved.

Save your skin.

There He is. The man, Jesus.

I heard Him speak a couple of times. Made perfect sense until He started on about loving your enemy and forgiveness. He probably doesn't have an enemy to forgive. A soldier hits Him with his club. My brain freezes. My heart stops... Then again, maybe He does.

I watch Him stagger. Then He sees me. He gives me a slight nod and a twitch of recognition until a push from behind sends Him to His knees. I empty my gut right there on the street.

It could be me.

They take Him — drag Him away. I have to follow. I pull my shawl tighter over my head and limp in the shadows at the edge of the mob. There is a shout and a man is ordered to carry the cross. He's a strong looking fellow, but even he stumbles under the weight.

The mob follows.

I follow.

Golgotha.

The Place of the Skull.

There they throw Jesus down onto the cross.

I have to go —

I have to leave —

I stay.

Then the hammering begins.

It could be me.

Crash! Crash! Crash!

I block my ears… Curl into a ball.

Crash! Crash!

Something roots me to the spot.

Fascination?

Intrigue?

Fear?

Shame?

It could be me.

I don't know how long I stand clenching my fists, my eyes, my toes… but a familiar voice breaks my turmoil.

'If You are the Christ, save Yourself and us.'

Ahab?

Then I realise there are two others hanging on crosses, one on either side of the man Jesus. I only recognise Ahab by his voice. His bloodied face and body could belong to any poor soul. Ahab had always been a smart-alecky jerk — just because he was named after a king. What had he done to deserve this?

Another voice gasps, rasps. 'Lord, remember me when You come into Your kingdom.' He, too, is unrecognisable. My gut spasms. My heart leaps. My throat closes over. No man deserves to be treated like this.

It could be me.

It should be me.

The Romans laugh.

Jesus takes a ragged breath. I spin towards Him. 'Assuredly,' He answers the man, 'today you will be with Me in Paradise.' He raises His eyes... towards me. Those eyes! I can't look away, even after He closes them in pain.

'Father,' he rasps and swallows. 'Forgive them.'

I stare open mouthed. *Forgive them?*

Jesus takes another ragged breath. 'They don't know what they're doing.'

Then He looks at a little group of women huddling and supporting each other. Shawls clutched to their chests. One woman stands strong — His mother?

What would it be like to know your mother?

I could barely remember mine. She had been murdered when I was four. Amma was pregnant and sick in bed. Some Roman soldiers forced their way into our house. My hands clenched at the unbidden memory. Abba had tried to stop them. I learnt a lesson that day. Romans have no scruples, no morals, no soul.

Jesus must be bursting with pain and dehydration. Even now, He cares for his mother.

A motley group of men and women, grief-stricken and weeping, huddle together a little way off, eyes haggard, mouths open in disbelief. His followers, I presume. I can feel their pain. Strange, because others' pain or discomfort rarely affects me.

What's happening to me? Am I becoming soft? I square my shoulders and look away. I am Barabbas, King of the Underworld. I take a sharp breath. *Was* King of the Underworld. Now I'm just Barabbas, mesmerised by a dying man with eyes of fire.

A ripple of power shakes Jesus. 'My God, My God, why have You forsaken Me?'

I may be a thief and a murderer, but even I know some Scripture. That's the beginning of one of David's psalms. Although I can't remember much of it, I do recall a bit. Why is He bringing it to our attention?

They pierce my hands and feet.

My face burns in shock. It can't be.

I can count all my bones. I mutter. Staring at the near-lifeless body in front of me, my mouth continues unassisted.

They look and stare at me.

They divide my garments among themselves

And for my clothing they cast lots.

Then, utter darkness swallows us all. The air is squeezed from the world.

People scream. Fear grips my chest, paralyses my body. I drop to the ground, clutching my knees, not wanting to stay, not wanting to look, not able to move. The darkness surrounds me — smothers me — suffocates me. I huddle into a senseless ball. I don't know for how long. It feels like hours.

My legs are numb. My hands clenched hard. My eyes blinded by the sudden return of light.

I hear him whisper. 'Father.' Then a feeble attempt to clear his throat. A shuddering breath and his ragged voice cries out, 'It is finished. Father, into your hands I commit my spirit.'

His eyes roll. His body goes limp. His lungs empty. I know he's dead.

Most onlookers have left. Not me. Something holds me.

Something connects me to this dead man. His followers kneel, shell-shocked and weeping. One looks up at me. I lower my eyes… retreat under my shawl.

The tramping of Roman feet disturbs the reverent hush.

The crack of broken bones. Ahab's scream. Another crack. Another shriek. I retch. Bile burns my throat.

'This one's already dead.'

'Weakling! Make sure of it!'

Horrified, I watch a soldier shove a spear into Jesus' heart. I could have told them He was dead. I've seen a lot of dead men in my life… many dead by my own hands. I know a dead man when I see one.

Jesus is dead. His blotched skin tells me His blood has already coagulated. Just to prove it, blood and water gush from his side.

A strange feeling rushes through me. Guilt? Shame? I've had the occasional regret at taking a life, but never have I felt guilty. What is happening to me?

I untangle my legs and stand, then fall to my knees.

Who are You?

Based on Matthew 27:20–51
Mark 15:7–40
Luke 23:18–49
John 19:15–37

Heartbeat

Dusty weary feet walked a thousand miles.
Dusty weary feet, bringing hope and smiles.
Dusty weary feet, treading rocks and stone,
Marching through the ages.
Calling forth His own.

Gracious loving hands hold children
on His knee.
Gracious loving hands cause the blind to see.
Gracious loving hands raised in
fervent prayer,
Seeking strength from Father God
For the pain He came to bear.

Dusty weary feet, tender loving hands
Pierced with nails of rusty iron.
They crucified Judah's Lion

On a cross.

A heartbeat,
A breath,
Jesus conquered death!
He rose again,
Victorious.

A heartbeat,
A breath,
Jesus conquered death!

Rusty iron could never stop

The King of Zion.

He didn't stop at the cross.
He didn't stop in the grave.
He didn't stop in the tomb.

In a tomb there's no room for life!

Papa's Journey

The funny thing about going on a journey is that
you usually tend to gather others along the way
Papa's journey involved all of us —
Mama, Alexander and me.
Every step Papa took us led to another discovery —
Then another —
And yet another.

Every corner, every crossroad led to the same
question.
What if Papa hadn't been forced to carry
the cross?
And every time the answer was the same.
All our lives —
mine
and yours
would have been different
— so very, very different.

Papa's Journey

PAPA RUBBED HIS RIGHT SHOULDER — yet again. His eyes glazed over.

I signalled to Alexander and together we slipped outside to tend the animals. Alexander sighed as he heaved the sheep-gate open. 'It's going to be another one of those long, silent evenings.'

Alexander was fifteen when we started this journey, and although younger than me by nearly two years, he was just as tall. Many people took us for twins — not identical twins, though. My hair is brown like Mama's. Alexander has inherited Papa's dark hair and heavy build. We've always been very close. We can share our deepest feelings and thoughts and know our secrets are safe with each other.

That evening started out the same as many of recent times — Papa's silent mood, Mama's worried eyes, animals that needed tending.

The sweet smell of hay greeted us as we set to work. 'I'm really worried, Rufus.' Alexander stopped pitching hay into the pen. 'Papa hasn't been the same since we got home from celebrating Passover.'

'I know. Mama says he'll be fine, but I can see the anxious look in her eyes.'

'What can we do?'

'Nothing.'

'Nothing? Come on, Rufus. There must be something! Maybe we could talk to Uncle Jacob.'

'Mama's already been to see Uncle Jacob and Uncle Benjamin.'

'Well, I guess we just have to pray and wait till Papa's ready to talk.'

I shook my head. 'Pray? Sure. You go ahead, Alexander. I wonder sometimes if God actually hears us.'

A shadow crossed the door of the barn. I swung around in horror.

'Papa! ... I didn't mean that... I didn't know you were there... I mean...'

I felt papa's strong hand on my shoulder. 'It's okay, Son. It's okay to question things as long as you look for your answers in the right places.'

I looked into my father's brown eyes and saw a clarity there I hadn't seen in weeks. He squeezed my shoulder and smiled 'Finish up in here, boys. Then come inside. There is something I need to discuss with you.'

Papa turned and strode out of the barn.

'Wow,' breathed Alexander. 'Did you see that? Papa smiled. He hasn't smiled since we were in Jerusalem for Passover.'

I was too stunned to answer.

Alexander and I entered the house and each sat on an embroidered cushion. Mama had made them — a blue one for me and a green one for Alexander. I traced my finger around the neat outline of white sheep lovingly embroidered around the edge. My cushion was part of my life. Even at seventeen, I could not think of sitting anywhere else.

I had no idea what Papa wanted to discuss and, frankly, I was rather alarmed. He had barely spoken for weeks.

Papa didn't seem to notice our entrance but sat staring once more into the distance. Then he sighed and looked us each in the eye — first Mama, then me, then Alexander.

'You know,' he began. 'I have been doing a lot of thinking. So much has happened... So much has happened.' Papa's voice trailed off.

Alexander gripped my arm.

Papa shook his head, took a deep breath and let it out very slowly. 'What if I hadn't been on the road at that very minute? What if I had started out five minutes earlier or five minutes later? What if I had walked a little faster or slower? What if we had been staying on the other side of Jerusalem or if a whim had taken me to go in at another gate? What if the centurion's eye had not chanced to alight on me in the crowd, or if he had picked out somebody else to carry the cross?'

'Ahh ... The cross... the cross.' Mama sounded so tired. 'Simon, people are being crucified every day. Why is this one so different?'

'Because... I looked into His eyes.' Papa stared at the ceiling, and for an instant, I thought he was going to retreat into wherever he had been going for the last few weeks. 'I looked into His eyes... They were so... so pure.' Papa's voice broke. 'And... He thanked me. He thanked me and blessed me for helping Him carry His cross.'

'Oh, Simon!' Mama crossed the room and placed her hands on Papa's strong, broad shoulders. I had never noticed how tiny Mama's hands were — or maybe it was just that Papa's shoulders were so broad. Mama's hands barely seemed to make an indent as she massaged his shoulders. Yet, he leaned into her and closed his eyes.

A pained expression crossed his face. 'I stayed; you know. I stayed and watched them crucify Him.'

I gasped and could feel Alexander tense beside me.

'You know they gambled for His clothes... at the foot of His cross... while He was gasping for breath... they were gambling for His clothes.'

Papa cleared his throat. His voice rasped. 'He died before they came to break His legs. They pierced His side with a spear to make sure He was dead. His blood had already congealed. Blood and water gushed out.'

'Simon, please! The boys!'

'They are no longer boys, Miriam.' Papa squeezed Mama's hand and looked into my eyes. 'They are almost grown men — old enough to hear and question their faith.'

My ears burned. I dared not move.

'Do you know what He said as they nailed Him to the cross?'

Mama was weeping now, and neither Alexander nor I were able to speak.

Papa's voice was barely a whisper. 'He said, "Father, forgive them. They know not what they do." He... interceded for... their forgiveness...' Papa broke down and wept.

I stared dumfounded into my brother's eyes. We had never seen Papa weep. It was too much. I grabbed Alexander's arm and we rose from the floor.

'Don't go... I need to finish.'

'Simon. Not now.' Mama's voice broke. 'We can speak about it another time.'

'No... No... I need to finish now.' Papa swallowed. 'I need to finish.'

Alexander and I slipped back onto our cushions. I didn't know where to look and I could feel Alexander's discomfort equalled mine.

Papa's voice regained its strength. 'Do you remember the sudden darkness that dropped over the earth that day?' Papa surveyed each of us as we stared transfixed. 'That happened while He hung on the cross... when He cried, "My God, My God. Why have You forsaken Me?" It was almost as if God couldn't look at Him hanging there.'

'What?' Alexander and I stared at each other.

'Yes. The world went black for three hours.' Papa stared into space and cleared his throat. 'Then

He died... and do you know what happened at that precise moment?'

Papa continued without waiting for an answer.

'The veil in the temple was torn in two... from top to bottom! From top to bottom! No man could have possibly done that.' Papa leant forward and whispered. 'So, who do you think did it?'

He didn't seem to want an answer. To tell the truth, I doubt I would have been able to answer. My throat was constricted, my body frozen.

'I have been doing a lot of thinking.' Papa's voice began to waver again.

I still wasn't game to look at him for fear of seeing the pain in his eyes.

Papa cleared his throat. 'I think His cry was pointing us all to the psalms. Rufus, fetch the Scriptures please.'

I glanced at Mama. She nodded, so I rose to collect the scrolls. There were not many people with copies of the writings, but Papa had transcribed the scripts with his strong, neat handwriting when he was in Jerusalem many years ago. I passed the scroll to Papa. Somehow, they looked like they belonged in his big sturdy hands.

'Read, please, Alexander.'

Alexander's eyes nearly popped out of his head. 'Me? But Papa, you always read the Scriptures.'

'Not today, Son. Read from here, please.'

Alexander swallowed and began to read.

For dogs have surrounded Me;

The congregation of the wicked has enclosed Me.

They pierce My hands and My feet;

I can count My bones.

They look and stare at Me.

They divide My garments among them
  and for My clothing they cast lots.

Alexander looked at me. I'm sure our puzzled expressions mirrored one another.

'Well done, Son. Now think about what I told you of the crucifixion I witnessed.'

Alexander frowned. 'They pierced His hands and His feet?'

'Yes. Yes. What else? ... Rufus?'

'You said they gambled for His clothes.'

'Yes! Yes! Exactly... just as David foretold...'

They divide My garments among them and for My clothes they cast lots.

'See! It's written right here! Now Rufus, your turn to read.'

Papa was beginning to get rather excited, and I was beginning to get more than a little scared, but I read the verse Papa pointed to.

He guards all His bones. Not one of them is broken.

Papa's eyes were wild with excitement. 'Don't you see? They didn't break His legs like they did to the others. David prophesied this too! It's all there... in the Scripture!'

I could sense Mama's alarm. I think it was easier when Papa was in his shell staring into nothing.

'Simon, please.'

'Just one more, Miriam... or maybe two.' He grinned and winked at Mama. She rolled her eyes and shook her head.

Papa's eyes twinkled. 'I'm reading this one. But first, I need to tell you about the trial.'

'The trial?' Alexander's curiosity shone in his eyes.

'This man, Jesus, was betrayed by one of His friends and sold for thirty pieces of silver.'

Mama gasped. 'What friend would do that?'

'Exactly. Nevertheless, it happened. Not only did it happen, but Zechariah prophesied that it would. He declared the word of the Lord, saying,

'If you think it best, give me my pay: but if not, keep it. So, they paid me thirty pieces of silver.'

'Oh, my,' gasped Mama.

Papa continued. 'Jesus was taken to be judged, but no one could agree on what He had done wrong. Finally, He was taken to Pilate who offered to set Him free as the yearly prisoner exchange — but the crowd was stirred up, and that's when they decided to crucify Him.' Papa's face clouded over. 'They didn't just crucify Him. First, they beat Him and pulled out His beard and spat on Him and mocked Him. They even made a crown of thorns and rammed it on His head.'

Mama gasped. I felt sick. Alexander stared at Papa as though he was a ghost.

'I'm sorry, but I need to explain everything. Remember what was written by the written by the prophet Isaiah? It's right here. Listen.

'I gave my back to those who struck me and my cheeks to those who plucked out the beard. I did not hide my face from shame and spitting.'

'How did Isaiah know that was going to happen?' Alexander was incredulous.

'Exactly,' continued Papa. 'How did he know? Except that God told him. Why did God tell him? That's the question we need to ask.'

My curiosity was strumming. 'Didn't they crucify Him with others, Papa? How do we know it was Him that Isaiah was talking about?'

'Now you are thinking, Son! Jesus was crucified between two thieves.'

'And?'

'And when He had died, He was placed in a grave of a rich friend.'

'And?'

'Read for yourself, Rufus. It's here.'

I stared at Papa. 'How can it be all there? Isaiah lived hundreds of years ago.'

'Read,' Papa commanded, opening the scroll and pointing. 'From here.'

So, I read.

'He was oppressed and He was afflicted,
Yet, He opened not His mouth.

He was led as a lamb to the slaughter.

And they made His grave with the wicked but with the rich at His death, because He had done no violence nor was any deceit in His mouth.'

The chills that crept up and down my spine almost made me collapse. Mama began to weep again and Alexander's mouth hung like a gaping cave. 'Who was this man?' Mama whispered.

'It's your turn to read, Miriam.'

Alexander and I stared at each other. Mama never read the scrolls.

'Simon... I...'

'Miriam, please...' He unrolled the parchment, scanning the text. 'This section here... from Isaiah again.'

Mama's hand trembled as she took the sacred scroll from Papa.

'For a child will be born to us, a son will be given to us; and the government will rest on His shoulders; and His name will be called Wonderful Counsellor, Mighty God, Eternal Father, Prince of Peace. There will be no end to the increase of His government or of peace, on the throne of David and over His kingdom, to establish it and to uphold it with justice and righteousness from then on and forevermore. The zeal of the Lord of hosts will accomplish this.'

Mama clutched the scrolls to her chest. 'This is the one,' she whispered. 'The one the prophecies are written about! The Messiah!' Fresh tears rolled down her cheeks.

Papa's eyes were glistening. Alexander and I stared from parent to parent and then back at each other.

I fell to my knees. 'The Messiah!' Every fibre in my being quivered with excitement. Without a shadow of doubt, I believed.

'We must go to Jerusalem,' Mama whispered. 'All of us.'

Papa grinned. 'If we leave in two days, we'll all be there in time for the Feast of Pentecost.'

I could almost see the plans forming in Mama's head — lists of things to pack and food to prepare. 'I'll be ready,' she whispered. A fresh gleam shone in her eyes. She swung around and embraced Papa. 'I'll be ready.'

Alexander and I grinned at each other.

Jerusalem!

Based on Matthew 27:32
Luke 23:26
Mark 15:21

The Beggar

Sometimes when hope is all you've got,
Hope is all you need.
Sometimes when faith is all you can grab,
Faith is all you need.
Sometimes when Love is all you need,
It comes.
Faith, Hope and Love.
But the greatest of these
Is Love.

The Beggar

'GET OUT OF THE WAY, beggar!'

Anger flared in my gut. I swivelled around and hurried back towards the ruckus. I knew only too well the scene I would find. Sure enough, there on the ground lay a beggar, splayed in the dirt, clutching his shawl, groping for his begging bowl. A rabble of young toughs surrounded him, snickering and jeering. One kicked dirt into his face.

When I glared at them, they took off like frightened cockroaches.

'I'm so sorry,' I whispered, touching the beggar's shoulder.

He flinched at my touch. 'What do you want? Here to mock me too?'

'No, friend. I'm here to help.'

The man lifted his head towards me. 'Why should you care?' Empty white eyes rolled in their sockets. Tears streaked tracks of mud down his dusty face.

Needles of tears stung my own eyes. Tears of anger at the undisciplined boys, tears of frustration at the injustice of the world, tears of sympathy. I squatted down and held his hands. He tried to pull away. Rearranging his beggar's shawl, I pressed his bowl into his hand, raised him to his feet and set his stick into his left hand.

'Why are you doing this?' His voice cracked with emotion.

I took his right elbow. 'I'm about to eat. Come and join me.' I was glad he couldn't see my own tears.

It wasn't very long ago I was in the exact same place. Dirty, hungry, blind, ridiculed, shunned. I could go on and on about my past. Sometimes I wonder how I managed to keep living… but we do. We humans do. We hold on because there's nothing else to do but breathe. When there is no hope, no sign of change, no food, no one to care, some glimmer crosses our paths and it's that glimmer that empowers the next days, the next weeks of life.

'Where are you taking me?' The fear in the beggar's question stirred me from my musings.

'We're going to my house. Trust me.' My voice threatened to betray me.

The man stumbled on beside me. I slowed my pace, remembering the feel of sharp stones on bare feet and the fear of stumbling through a dark unfamiliar void. 'Nearly there, friend. We just need to climb this rise.' I gripped his hand and helped him up the path to my house.

'Where are we going?' Panic crept into his voice.

'To my house,' I answered. 'There's no need to fear.' I doubted he believed me.

At the top of the rise, the dusty path gave way to soft grass. The beggar stopped and wriggled his feet in the cool damp. I lowered him onto a rock and held his shoulder, remembering the fear of being left in unfamiliar surroundings. That had been one of the despicable tricks the village thugs played on me... picked me up, carried me away and dropped me. I'm sure my new friend had been bullied in the same way. 'I'm still here.' I squeezed his shoulder. 'I won't leave you alone.'

At the crunch of footsteps on the gravel path, the beggar whimpered. I held his shoulder. 'You have nothing to fear. It's my servants.' Ezra arrived carrying a big bowl. Matthias limped behind with a pitcher of water. I bent in front of the beggar and put his feet into the bowl. He pulled back, nearly falling off the rock. 'Trust me,' I whispered. I took his feet again and nodded to Matthias to pour the water over them.

'Why are you doing this?' the man gasped.

'We all need a friend,' I answered using a cloth to slosh cool water over his feet and legs. I let his feet soak. 'My name is Bartimaeus.'

'You're Bartimaeus? The blind man from the gate? The man who was healed by the Rabbi?'

'Yes. That's me. Guilty as charged.' I motioned Matthias to bring another bowl for the man's hands. He plunged them deep into the cool water. A smile played on his lips. I imagined those muscles hadn't had a work out for a long time.

'Wash your arms, friend. Here's a towel.'

The man stopped. 'So, you know... you know what it's like.' He cleared his throat. Tears dribbled down his beard. 'How can you do this to me, then? It would have been better to leave me in the street. I'll just... have to go back.'

I squeezed his shoulders. 'No, my friend. No, you won't. Do you have a name?'

'I used to,' he answered. 'Now I'm just Beggar or Scum.'

My heart swirled with memories. My gut clenched with indignation. My vision blurred. 'What's your name?'

'It used to be Obadiah,' he replied. Blank white eyes raised to meet mine.

'Here,' I whispered placing a clean tunic in Obadiah's hands. 'I can smell our dinner is ready. When you're dressed Matthias will bring you inside.'

'Do you have any more water?' his voice croaked.

'We have plenty but it's cold.'

'Is it clean?'

'Yes. It's clean,'

'Good,' he grinned, ripping off his rags and pouring the bowl of water over his head. Brown rivers streaked down his skinny, malnourished body. 'You're right,' he laughed. 'It's cold.'

'Matthias will help you with more water,' I chuckled. 'And there's plenty of soap.' 'Bring Obadiah into the house when he's ready, Matthias.'

The man who shuffled into the house was almost unrecognisable. His face glowed. Gone was the dust from his beard and hair. Gone were the cakes of mud from his legs and arms. In their place was man with a wide toothless grin and a questioning mind.

Obadiah was keen to hear what had happened to me since I was in his position — blind, hungry, alone, despised. He'd been hiding behind a cart the day Jesus healed me, too scared to move, too scared to join me.

'I regret my cowardliness every day,' he whispered, head in his hands. 'Every day, I wish I'd had the courage to call out. Every day…' He raised his white eyes to where he thought I was sitting. 'What happened to you? I heard you left Jericho.'

'I spent two years travelling with Jesus. He healed the sick, blessed the children, preached and loved everyone. He was so wise and patient right to the end.'

'The end?' Obadiah frowned.

'They crucified Him.' I said simply.

'Why? Everything I heard about Him was so positive. People flocked to Him when He came.'

'Ignorance. Jealousy.'

'That's too bad.' Obediah muttered. 'People were hoping He was the Messiah come to save Israel. All is lost.'

'He was the Messiah, but not the way everyone thought. All is not lost. In fact, everything is perfect.

He rose again from the dead. I saw Him with my own eyes.'

'How? That's impossible! How can a man rise from the dead?'

'Because,' I answered. 'Because, He is the Son of God, sent to earth for our salvation. Let me read to you. Matthias, pass the scrolls.' I read from Isaiah and Jeremiah and the psalms.

Emotions passed over Obadiah's face like waves. Wonder, awe, confusion, delight, fear, curiosity. He sat entranced. 'No one has ever explained that to me. I guess no one ever wanted to get close enough to me for anything, let alone believe I was worthy of hearing the Scriptures.'

I motioned for Matthias to serve the dates and wine and let Obadiah ponder over what I had told him.

'Can I be baptised?' he whispered. He dropped his head. 'I guess not. I'm unclean.'

'Baptism is for everyone,' I answered. 'There's more... healing is for everyone too.'

'But you told me Jesus has died and gone to the Father.' He shook his head. 'I guess I missed out.'

'No, Obadiah, you didn't miss out. Nobody did. After Jesus died, we were terrified. Terrified of the Romans, but more so of the Pharisees. Early one morning, we were praying, a hundred and twenty of us, crammed into an upper room. I don't know how to explain it, but fire from Heaven came down and landed on each of us.'

'Did it burn?'

I laughed. 'No. It was glorious. Many times, I've tried to relive that marvellous morning. The colours. The power. The peace. Jesus sent the Holy Spirit… We were immersed in the Holy Spirit of God.' I cleared my throat. Emotions threatened to choke me. 'Before He left this earth, Jesus told us to go into all the world and baptise. He said we must do what He did and we would even do more wonders than He did.'

Obadiah shook his head. 'How could any man heal anyone?'

'That's the point. No man can, but with the power of God's Spirit, in the name of Jesus, we can.'

'Are you telling me you could heal me?'

'No. I can't.'

Obadiah's face fell. All the excitement and hope and expectation dissolved. His shoulders dropped. He held his head in his hands. A sob escaped his throat.

I held his shoulder. 'But Jesus can. If you're open to His Spirit.'

He raised his chin. A new light, a spark, a glimmer of hope radiated from his expectant face. 'I am,' he whispered, stumbling to his feet. 'The Scriptures you read cannot be wrong.'

'Right then,' I grinned, placing my hands on his head. I knew God would hear me. I prayed and I felt Obadiah shake beneath my hands.

Even before I had finished, he moved and stumbled towards a wall. He frowned at the brass pot hanging on the hook. 'My hair is a mess!' He doubled over, gripping his stomach. 'Thank you! Thank you!' Like a child with a new toy, a boy with a raisin bun, a bird with a crust of bread, Obadiah danced and laughed.

'Thank you!' he cried.

'Don't thank me,' I exclaimed.

'I'm not,' Obadiah grinned. He stared at the pot again. 'Do you have a razor?'

Based on Matthew 28:18–20
Mark 16:15–18
Luke 24:46–49

Martha's Secret

I'll never forget His eyes!
— How glorious —
— full of fire —
Yet so peaceful.
They stared straight into me —
Through me.
Into the depths of my soul,
Into my spirit.

Martha's Secret

'TELL ME YOUR BIGGEST SECRET.' Simon's eyes sparkled with mischief.

'What?'

'Your biggest secret,' Simon repeated. 'I know you have a secret. Something has changed in you.'

I stared past him. 'Nothing's changed.'

'Martha, we've known each other for eleven years — since we were babies. Come on... what is it?'

I really liked Simon. Fortunately, we were still young enough for our friendship to be innocent, but sometimes — sometimes, I dream of his big brown eyes and imagine being lost in the depths of their softness. *I wonder what it would be like to have him look at me the way Joshua looks at my cousin?*

'What are you smiling about, Martha? Must be some secret.'

I gasped and shook my head. *Dare I tell him?* I spun around and looked him straight in the eye. 'Okay. You're right. Something did happen.'

'I knew it!' Simon lay back on the grass with his hands behind his head, smug look on his face. 'Well, come on,' he teased.

I took a deep breath and held it for a few seconds. 'I died last year.'

'Oh, funny girl.' Simon rolled onto his stomach. 'You died. Yeah, sure, Martha.'

'It was glorious, Simon! The colours! The music! Sometimes I lie awake at night trying to recapture it all — but I can't.' I glanced at Simon. His throat was jumping up and down. His mouth hung open. I turned away. 'Well, you did ask!'

There was no answer.

'Simon, I'm telling the truth.' I jumped to my feet. 'But if you don't believe me — fine!' I stomped off with the biggest show I could muster.

'Hey, Martha, wait up.' Simon's breath was in my ear. He grabbed my arm. 'I'm sorry,' he breathed. 'That wasn't the sort of secret I was expecting.'

The rage threatening to choke me subsided. I never had been able to stay angry with Simon for long. 'Yeah, well, I guess it is kind of hard to believe.' I spun around to face him. 'But it really did happen, Simon. I really did die.'

'How? I mean — you died? Died... like dead?'

'Of course I "died like dead" — is there any other sort of "died"?'

This was the first time I'd spoken to anyone outside my own family about that day. I was regretting my decision, but figured I'd come too far to opt out now. Besides, this was Simon. We'd shared secrets since I could remember. I took a deep breath. 'Remember last year when I got sick?'

'That was a bad time.' Simon stared into the distance. 'Lots of people got sick.' I could see him close his eyes and swallow. 'That's when Jare...' Simon stopped walking. He spun around to face me. Pain contorted his face. I wished I could say something — do something — to help. He turned away. 'You know, Martha,' Simon spoke to the air. 'Sometimes I wish Jared had died instead of... Martha, he can't do anything — can't feed himself, can't dress himself... can't even.'

My throat tightened. Jared had been like a big brother to me as well as to Simon. Our families shared meals on top of each other's houses in the summer months. We even built our sukkot next to each other.

'Amma's so weary these days,' Simon whispered. 'I don't know what to do. Jared's too heavy for me to lift. I hate seeing Amma struggling and Abba works long hours and doesn't get home 'til late.' He cleared his throat. 'If it wasn't for your family, I don't know what we'd do.' Simon dragged his hand across his face leaving a dirty smudge.

I steered him to a tree and we sat in the shade. The village became a blur through my tears. Guilt washed over me. I pulled my knees up under my chin. *Why was I healed and not Jared?* Simply because my Amma asked Jesus to heal me. It was as simple as that.

Anyhow Jared wasn't very sick when Jesus passed through Bethphage.

'I'm sorry Martha. Tell me what happened.'

I stared into the distance. The spring sunlight danced on the stones of the village wall. The midday haze played on the rooftops. 'Sometimes I lie awake at night and try to remember.' I whispered to the breeze. 'The tenderness and the power... I heard a voice reverberating through my spirit. It was inside me and outside me at the same time. "Little girl, wake up." Then a tingling warmth started from my hands and spread through my body.' I swung to face Simon. 'Try as I might, I can't recapture it.'

'It really happened — like that?'

I nodded. 'I know I heard it — felt it... And His eyes! I will never forget them — so glorious — full of fire — yet so peaceful. They stared straight into me — into the depths of my soul.'

Simon was silent for a while. 'Martha, you know they killed Him,' he whispered.

'Killed who?'

'Jesus. They killed Him.'

My heart lurched. 'What?'

'They killed Him.'

'Who killed Him?'

Simon scratched in the dirt. 'The Scribes and Pharisees.'

'Why?'

'Abba says they were jealous of Him because He taught with authority and pointed out ways they were not keeping God's message.'

New tears streamed down my face. 'I don't believe it!'

'It's true. It happened at Passover.'

I could feel my chest convulsing. I gasped for breath.

'I'm sorry, Martha. I thought you knew. You know they say He came back to life.'

I lifted my head and stared at Simon, aware of the anguish on my face. 'What?'

'They say He came back to life.'

'Where is He now?'

'I'm not sure, but heaps of people say they've seen Him.'

'Simon, we have to find Him. We have to ask Him to heal Jared. Don't you see? He can heal Jared!' I grabbed Simon's hand and pulled him up. 'Come on!'

'Martha, He died!'

I stepped right up to Simon's face. 'So did I.'

Simon's brown skin paled. His eyes stilled. 'Come on!' He grabbed my hand and together we ran to the village.

I burst through the open door and ran straight into my father. 'Abba! They killed Jesus!'

'Whoa!' I felt Abba's strong arms around me and I struggled against them. It was no use. I gave up struggling and fell into his chest, sobbing. He held me close. His steady heart beat soon calmed me. 'Martha,' he whispered into my hair.

'Why didn't you tell me?'

Abba exchanged strange glance with Amma. She sighed. 'We didn't want you to be upset.'

I hugged Abba and straightened up on his lap. 'You're right. I would have been upset, but you hear He came back to life?'

'Where did you hear that?'

'Simon told me. He said heaps of people have seen Him.'

Amma knelt down in front of me. 'Martha, I guess you really need to hear the whole story.' She glanced at Papa again. 'Jesus was betrayed by one of the Twelve.'

'What? Who would do that?'

'It was Judas,' Abba whispered.

'Judas?' I swallowed. 'Why?'

'Some say greed. But he couldn't bear the guilt so he... killed himself.'

'Judas? Killed himself?' I fell back against Papa's chest. Judas was a friend of my Uncle James.

A new determination rose within me. 'We have to find Him. We have to find Jesus!'

Papa frowned. 'We already thanked Him for healing you, Martha.'

'You don't understand, Abba.' My voice squeaked. 'He can heal Jared!'

'Martha…' Amma patted my cheek. 'Jared can't walk or talk.'

'Yes, Amma... and I was dead!'

Abba stood up so fast I almost tumbled off his lap. 'I'll be right back.' His voice was hoarse and I could see his eyes shining as he hurried out the door.

'Martha, you're amazing!' Amma swooped down and hugged me tight. 'Come and help me. I promised Joanna I'd make dinner for her family. She has given me vegetables to cook. Eli's not home from work yet and Jared's having a bad day.'

Soon, the aroma of chopped herbs and hearty vegetables filled the kitchen. My heart was singing. I knew Jesus would heal Jared. We just had to find him.

'Mmm, that smells good!' Abba's big frame filled the doorway. His white teeth sparkled above his beard.

'What have you been up to, Josiah?' Amma pointed the wooden stirring spoon at Abba. 'Don't just stand there like a grinning donkey.' Abba's big, muscular arms encircled her and the spoon. I hadn't realised how small Amma was 'til then. Her arms didn't even make it around Abba's middle.

A shadow crossed the doorway. Simon's abba, Eli — face blotchy, tears streaming down his face, stumbled through the door. 'Do you really think Jared can be healed?' he whispered. I could see his jaw working hard.

'Eli, come in.' Abba led our dear friend to a stool. Eli sat heavily and rested his head in his hands. 'We know Jesus can heal Jared,' said Abba, resting his big hand on our friend's shoulder. 'I don't know why we didn't think of it before.'

Eli looked up. His eyes were heavy-rimmed and weary. 'We've been to all the doctors.' His voice quavered. 'They said nothing can be done... and this paralysis often happens when someone has a bad fever. Usually...' Eli swallowed. '... children die.' He glanced up at me and closed his eyes. 'Oh, Martha, I'm so sorry.'

'Uncle Eli, don't be sorry. That's exactly why we need to take Jared to Jesus. I died and He healed me. I know He can heal Jared.'

Eli shook his head. 'They killed Him,' he whispered.

'Yes.' I knelt down in front of Uncle Eli and took his rough hands in mine. 'But He came back to life.'

Uncle Eli looked into my eyes for a long time. I saw a glimmer of a twinkle, then his whole face lit up.

'So, it's settled?' Abba's voice boomed through the house.

'What's settled?' Amma and I spoke together.

'Jerusalem. We're all going to Jerusalem. Tomorrow.'

'Tomorrow?' Amma gasped. 'Come *on*, Josiah! We need to prepare and pack.'

'Well, then. The day after tomorrow. We'll be in Jerusalem for Pentecost.'

Uncle Eli stood and hugged me. He smelt of leather and polish. I loved that smell. I knew his hug was his thank-you. Then he hugged Abba. Together the two men danced a little jig. It was like Purim. They were so funny together.

'We'll be over as soon as dinner is cooked. I think this is a cause for celebration.'

We were up early the next morning. Amma and I spent the morning in the kitchen cooking up a storm and the afternoon packing things we would need for our journey. Just before sunset, Abba and Uncle Eli arrived with two carts and two scruffy donkeys.

'I hope these fellows live up to their owner's promise,' Abba muttered.

Although scruffy and rather smelly, the donkeys had the most beautiful eyes. I'm sure they understood every word, so I reassured them with a scratch behind their ears and a promise to watch over them. They waited patiently while Abba and Eli loaded our packages. By mid-morning we were off. Excitement bounced in my middle. Amma had helped me make a special date cake for Aunt Sara. I smiled to myself. I bet Uncle James tries to tease her and sneak some.

'We'll walk for a bit,' Abba announced, holding my hand. 'The donkeys will get enough of a workout once we reach the city walls.' I wondered if the donkeys were grateful. I was. I couldn't sit still.

'Come on, Martha,' Simon called racing past.

I looked to Abba. He laughed and nodded his head.

I took off, knowing I didn't have a hope of catching up to Simon but enjoying the freedom and the holiday breeze in the air. We waited a mile up the road, puffing and glowing with excursion. 'I don't remember the road being this long and dusty,' I said, wiping my scarf over my forehead.

'Hasn't been any rain for a while,' Simon answered, handing me a juicy date.

It wasn't long before Jerusalem's wall towered above us. Then the climb began. Enthusiasm was forgotten.

I saw Simon glance back with a worried look on his face. 'I hope Jared's okay. The road is a lot bumpier than I remember.'

'And a lot steeper,' I added. 'I don't feel like we're getting anywhere.'

Excitement drowned in aching legs, we plodded on. In an instant, the road levelled and humanity swallowed us.

'My, I had forgotten how many people there are in the city,' Amma sighed.

'Pentecost always brings the crowds,' Eli answered. 'Stay close.'

I certainly didn't need to be told twice. In an instant, Abba lifted me into the little cart. Amma held me tight.

'Oh, Abba, the poor donkey. Can he pull us both?' My cry was lost in the hubbub.

Lambs bleated. Donkeys brayed. Stall holders cried out. Hagglers argued. Women called. Children played tag amongst the coloured booths.

Our faithful donkey, however, didn't flinch. His little head bobbed up and down following Abba. Every bump in the road made me cringe — not for my sake. My heart ached for Jared who was lying in the bottom of the cart in front. The road to Jerusalem had been very bumpy and very grimy.

'I wonder how Jared is handling all the noise.' I had to yell for Amma to hear me.

'My brother's house is just a few streets away. It shouldn't be as bad there.'

I nodded. It was no use trying to have a conversation amongst the clamour invading our sanity. The donkeys plodded on through the market place and around a corner. All of a sudden, we were in a different world. The only sound was the clip-clop of our donkeys' hooves.

Amma let out an audible sigh. I felt her relax against me. 'I don't understand why anyone would choose to live here.'

'Josiah! Lidia! Martha! How good to see you!'

Mama's eyes lit up.

'Uncle James!' I jumped down from the cart before it had even stopped and was instantly engulfed in Uncle James' bear-like arms. I loved Uncle James.

'Well, now who is this strapping young man? Can't be Simon. Simon's just a boy. Uncle James ruffled Simon's hair and greeted his parents. 'Run along inside, you two. Sara has dates and hot honey cakes.'

I grabbed Simon's hand, but not before I noticed worried looks pass between the adults as they moved towards Eli's cart.

Simon saw it too. He frowned. 'Jared hasn't had a very good trip,' he whispered. 'At least he can rest more comfortably now.'

It wasn't long before we were seated on cushions around the low table. Aunt Sara made cushions to sell at the markets. Blue ones and green ones, purple ones and red ones. I chose a purple one with little camels embroidered around the edge.

'My, this stew is good, Sara! Is it another new recipe?' Mama and Sara were forever exchanging recipes.

'I'll give it to you in the morning,' Sara smiled. 'Right now, judging by your yawns, I think it's time for bed.'

I was hoping everyone would be going to bed soon. I could hardly keep my eyes open but I didn't want to miss anything. Simon was already asleep on his abba's shoulder.

Strange, sounds, strange smells — shouting, donkey brays, wagon wheels and tramping feet woke me the next morning. I had almost forgotten the noises and smells a Jerusalem morning carries, but somehow, this morning, it didn't seem quite right. Frowning, I joined the others for breakfast. Eli kept glancing at the door and catching Abba's eye. Aunt Sarah stood as if listening for something. The donkeys brayed. Dogs barked. Abba frowned.

'What is it?' Amma whispered.

With a woosh, the window latches rattled. The front door swung open and the sound of a rushing wind churned in the air. Uncle James and Abba raced to the doorway. Eli joined them, then Simon. Not wanting to miss anything, I sidled close to Abba. His arm tightened around me.

Uncle James frowned. 'I've never heard anything like it.' He peered up and down the street. 'How strange.'

We watched for a moment, then Abba drew me inside. The bizarre sound of the wind filled the air, even after he closed the door.

Simon and I stared at each other. Simon's eyes were glassy. His skin paled and I wondered if I looked as scared. Abba held me tight... waiting.

Nothing happened. No storm — nothing — just a sound like a mighty wind.

'I can't imagine what it could be,' Abba said, peering back outside. 'Everyone's heading to the square. Come on, let's go and see.'

'Josiah? Is that wise?' Amma shrank back against the wall.

'We'll stay at the edge. Don't worry, Lidia. I feel at peace about this.'

'We're coming too!' Eli grabbed Simon's hand. 'Joanna and Sara are staying with Jared.'

Simon grinned at me. His hair was still tousled, his tunic askew. I shook my head.

'What's wrong, Martha?'

'I see you had honey cakes for breakfast.'

Simon wiped his face with the back of his hand and licked his fingers. 'Yeah,' he grinned. 'How'd you guess?'

Eli chuckled. It was so good to hear him laugh again.

We could hear the commotion long before we got to the square. I gripped Abba's hand with both of mine. Abba might have felt at peace but my heart was pounding.

Peter and the disciples were speaking — different languages! It seemed everyone could understand them — even the Egyptians!

Abba frowned. 'They certainly don't look drunk. Anyway, it's only the third hour.'

Peter's voice seemed too loud to be coming from one man. It filled the whole square. 'This Jesus, God has raised from the dead.'

My heart skipped a beat. A thousand ants crawled over my head. I clutched Abba's big hand tighter. There was no space to move. People filled every inch of the square yet Peter's voice could be heard over the top of everyone. 'Therefore, let the house of Israel know assuredly that God has made this Jesus whom you crucified both Lord and Christ.'

A great murmur arose. 'What shall we do?' someone called.

Peter raised his arms. 'Repent and let everyone of you be baptised in the name of Jesus the Christ for the redemption of sins and you shall receive the gift of the Holy Spirit.'

With a deafening cheer, the crowd began to move.

I tugged at Abba's hand. 'Where are they going?'

'I'm guessing to the Pool of Siloam.'

'I want to go too!' I told Abba.

'And me,' added Simon.

Papa, Eli and Uncle James held each other's gaze for a few seconds. Big grins broke out simultaneously.

Abba scooped me up and took Amma's hand. Uncle Eli held Simon's shoulder and grabbed Abba's cloak. We joined the throng.

Amongst the jostling and pushing and calling we somehow managed to stay together.

It seemed like hours before it was our turn. Hundreds of wet people sloshed past us, some crying, some laughing — all praising God. We were just about the last in the queue.

It was worth the wait. I will never forget that day! It was the most glorious thing — besides being raised from the dead, of course. I felt the same warmth, the same peace, the same joy.

When I came up from the water, I grabbed Peter's hand. 'Please. Where's Jesus? We need Him.'

'What do you know of Jesus, little one?'

I was nearly crying. 'We need Him.'

'Jesus has gone to heaven.' Peter's voice sounded like a hundred angels singing.

'But He can't have!' My voice cracked. 'We need Him! Simon's brother, Jared, got the same sickness I did… now he can't speak or feed himself,' My throat closed. 'Please,' I whispered. 'I know Jesus can heal him. I know He can.' I didn't let go of Peter's hand.

'How do you know that?'

My tears were flowing freely, mixing with the water dripping from my hair. 'Last year I died and... Jesus healed me.'

Peter looked into my eyes. I felt like I was swimming in love. 'Where is Jared?'

'At my uncle's,' I whispered.

Uncle Eli stepped forward. 'It's true, sir. Jesus raised this little girl. My son caught the same sickness and now...' Uncle Eli's voice faltered.

Peter tipped my chin up and looked deep into my eyes. A grin broke over his face. 'Take me to your friend, little one.'

Based on Acts 2

Building with Grace
— A Prayer for all Disciples

Gracious, loving Father, help me to see
That the future of our movement
Is up to me
and me,
and me,
and me,
and me.
Help us work together
With Grace and Harmony,
Building on foundations of the past.

Our future can't be built
Without a past to build upon.
Our future can't be built
Without mentors true and strong.
Our future can't be built
Without decisions wise and true.
Lord, our future can't be built without You.

There was someone there
When I was young and new.
There was someone there
To teach me what to do.
There was someone there—
And now I see
That the someone who is there
Is now me.

Gracious Loving Father I pray for strength.
And I pray for Your patience and Your grace.
And peace and the wisdom to let go.
Help us build together
with one accord,
So that we can move on forward,
Together build our future.
Let's move along and build with grace.

Our future can't be built
Without a past to build upon.
Our future can't be built
Without mentors true and strong.
Our future can't be built
Without decisions wise and true.
Lord, our future can't be built without You.

Choose Wisdom

The rest of your life is ahead of you.
Think wisely.
Choose Wisdom.

Some decisions will be easy.
Choose Wisdom.

Some will be fun.
Choose Wisdom.

Some will be hard.
Choose Wisdom.

Some will break your heart.
Seek wise counsel.
Choose Wisdom.

One day, we will all have to stand
before God
and give account of everything
we've said, thought and done.

Be ready,
Choose Wisdom.

About the Author

AUSTRALIAN AUTHOR JUDY ROGERS writes in a diverse range of genres.

In 2020 her unpublished children's fantasy manuscript, *The Farmyard Prince*, was shortlisted in the CALEB Awards.

Judy also writes poetry and has released a CD of fun and inspirational songs.

Judy is a retired primary Special Education teacher. She is also a leadership Trainer volunteering with Girl Guides Queensland. Judy enjoys gardening, painting, travelling and spending time with her children, ten grandchildren and two spoilt puppies. As a teacher, Judy encouraged her students to look beyond themselves and explore the world around them.

Her aim is to encourage others to step out of the box, to explore possibilities and to think big and wide and wild.

Acknowledgements

WITHOUT THE EXPERTIESE and patient guidance of Anne Hamilton from Armour Books, this dream would never have been realised. Thank you, Annie.

My sincere appreciation and thanks go to Beck Robinson from Beckon Creative for her bottomless imagination and inspiration.

To both friends — again, thank you for being so patient and kind.

No project can be accomplished without the support of family and friends. Thanks to my children and those who have encouraged me on this journey.